PIECES of LIFE

PIECES of LIFE
A collection of short works

Copyright © 2016 The Landfall Writers' Group

All rights reserved. No part of this book may be reproduced, stored, transmitted, or copied in any form, electronical or mechanical, including photocopying, recording or transmitting by any information and retrieval system, except by written permission of contributing author(s).

You may contact any of the authors at the following email address: LandfallWriters@gmail.com

Published by The Landfall Writers' Group

Printed by Blurb

Printed in the United States

Disclaimer: Each story contained in this book is based on the contributing author's recollections of events, related to the best of his or her knowledge. No errors, oversights or harm were intended for any individual, organization or company.

We would like to dedicate this collection to each of our readers and the writer that is within you. We encourage you to join us in telling your stories.

CONTENTS

Ed Hearn
    An Evening to Remember
    Alaskan Salmon at the Falls and Grizzly Bears
    Alaska Memories
    Magical Christmas
    There Really Is a Santa Claus
    A Morning of Enlightenment
    A Life-Changing Struggle to Survive
    A Fourth of July to Remember
    Fishing the Easy Way with Explosives
    Fishing Trip to Florida for Big Bass
    Getting to Know a Florida State Trooper
    Catching Crappie with Dad
    Surprising Dad While Fishing

Dick Nasca
    My Day at Prestwick Links
    Exit Delivery
    Grapes of Wrath
    Meeting Fortunata
    My Day at the Old Course at Saint Andrews
    Sharing the Fourth of July with My Animal Charges
    Train to Truckee
    Pink Jacket Covered with Blood
    Denver Christmas Blizzard of 1982
    Birthday Shutout

CONTENTS *continued*

Diane Torgerson
    From Another Galaxy
    Dancing with the Stars
    Memories
    Mimes
    Andy
    A Crime, Burglary and Pablum
    Laughter
    Seng
    Halloween Bunnies
    Mile Marker 462
    New Years Eve
    Oak Ridge, Tennessee: The Magic City
    Earthquake

Charlotte Hackman
    Bathroom Misunderstanding
    Bathroom Counseling
    The White Roses
    Getting "Unsquared"
    Butts and Bears

Marie Gillis
    A Revolutionary Fourth

John Roper
    HGTV

CONTENTS *continued*

Myrna Brown
    A Boy's Best Friend
    Family Ties

Sarah Giachino
    Exerpt from *Dearest Darling, Dearest Sweetheart*

Doris Chew
    Gung-Gung and Po-Po

Sherry Roberts Highberger
    The Witch of Chattoka
    My First Kiss

Ann Keeble
    Against Autumn's Sky

FORWARD

This collection of short works was written by a group of writers who started gathering in October of 2015 in Landfall, a gated community in Wilmington, North Carolina. The purpose of The Landfall Writers' Group is to establish a collaborative forum to share ideas and to provide constructive feedback for the creative efforts of the members in a positive venue. The group consists of writers with various skill levels and writing interests. Projects vary, including memoirs, family histories, fiction and non-fiction. Guest authors and editors are invited to share their expertise through seminars and workshops.

There have been four books and numerous magazine articles published by members of the group at the time of this printing. We hope you will see more of our work in the future. These little "pieces of life" are a sample of our creative efforts over the past year, and are presented for your enjoyment.

We all have our own unique stories to share. We encourage each of you to take time to record yours ... while you can still remember them!

The only writer to whom you should compare yourself is the writer you were yesterday.
David Schlosser

Ed Hearn was born in Nashville, Tennessee where he lived for his first fifty years. While there, he worked in a manufacturing/printing business for thirty years while serving as a part owner. He has now been retired for almost seventeen years and currently lives in the Landfall development located in Wilmington, North Carolina.

Ed enjoys golf, tennis, boating, fishing, traveling, creating sculpture of both wood and bronze, producing acrylic paintings and participating in Masters Track and Field competitions throughout the United States and around the world.

Recently, Ed joined the Landfall Writers' Group with a number of other local creative writers. He has been writing short stories and his memoirs for the past few years in an effort to share his life and experiences with both his family and other interested individuals. Most of his varied subject matter for these personal stories come from close observation of his surroundings, expressed with a touch of humor and philosophy.

AN EVENING TO REMEMBER
Ed Hearn

As we looked upward through the evening skies of crimson red and a wonderful gray-blue hue along the horizon, the familiar shape of a large, metallic object came into focus. It was traveling very fast and headed directly into the light breeze gently blowing over our heads. Huge wings allowed it to approach and float in the air like an eagle while a powerful engine propelled its forward progress. We were spellbound in this moment as the floatplane descended and lost altitude quickly on its approach to the crystal clear lake at our feet.

On this night, Alaska's Lake Hood was serene and peaceful. Its waters were already still and a large gray heron stood in the tall reeds at the edge waiting for its evening meal before the light faded to nothingness. The bird's movement was frozen as its gaze was focused downward to an area holding tiny fish unaware of their fate. The surface of the water only cast tiny ripples, which were reflecting like silver droplets that stretched the light toward us in long bands. Every few minutes a small fish would break the stillness to cause a distraction in the symmetry of this perfect place. This smooth world extended away from us in three different directions toward the thick, dark green evergreens bordering the shores in the distance.

We had temporarily been peaceful and relaxed but now the mechanical motor caused a noise that was deafening as the plane passed within thirty feet of our heads, causing a breeze that stirred our hair. On its long and graceful approach, we both wondered how far it would glide just above the surface before finally lightly touching the still waters. Small blinking lights on the wing's edge reflected off the water's surface, creating a double image as the plane entered the water and slid to a stop. The aircraft then turned and increased engine speed in an effort to reach its mooring position against one of the docks to the far side of the lake.

As we watched the plane move to the right, we wondered where it had been on this day in Alaska. Had this plane just completed a fishing excursion to an isolated stream in a faraway location? We were eager to find out what it was like to rise above the Arctic tundra and glide effortlessly over the snow-covered grasses and forests on the way to excitement. But at the moment, all we could do was fantasize about what we would experience in the next few weeks.

I reached down and lifted the bottle of red wine, filling two glasses to an appropriate level. The wooden bench where we sat was positioned perfectly to observe the evening sky and allowed us to watch the darkening sunset in a carefree manner as we sipped our merlot. We were alone and content; everything was again still and quiet.

As my mind slowed, I leaned back and stared up at the heavens. I was thankful for everything around me. The night air was cool and my mind was at rest. Eventually we headed back inside, but this time of enchantment was to be long remembered.

ALASKAN SALMON AT THE FALLS AND GRIZZLY BEARS
Ed Hearn

Walking up the deserted trail, which is covered by small gray stones and loose gravel, my mind drifts back to the float plane trip that had recently carried me to this moment in time.

While gliding over open expanses of space, I had observed the landscape below. Large grassy fields and thickly treed, green forests were separated by many streams and lakes, which wound through and dotted the countryside in all directions. The large lakes cast reflections of our plane as it progressed toward our destination.

Looking out the glass pane, I had felt as if I was hanging in the air, suspended by a thin line dropped down from heaven. The only sound was the constant hum of the powerful engines and the propeller was a dark blur a few feet in front of my eyes. I was free and my spirit had soared in tune with the aircraft, which transported me to the unknown.

In the distance was a large, blue lake formed by an ice glacier at the base of two, totally white, snow-covered mountains. The stillness of the water from my perspective made the surface appear to be a mirror casting images of the soft clouds from above. The ridges on either side were in sharp contrast and sloped steeply while falling directly into the silent beauty. Faint irregularities in the hillsides indicated valleys transporting the melted moisture from high above. This all blended together beautifully, but appeared more like a fairy tale than a location I was about to invade.

Then the machine had banked slightly and began its descent toward the stillness below. The edge of our landing area approached rapidly and I tensed slightly in anticipation. Air moving across the windowsill created a whistling noise, which could be heard over the shifting sound of the motor as we prepared for landing. I could feel my heart beating rapidly inside my chest and the inner excitement was intense, as was my focus.

The actual touchdown was anticlimactic, but we continued to glide swiftly over the smooth water until we came to an eventual halt near the middle of the lake. Once at rest, the engine speed was increased and we propelled our aircraft toward the far shore. Another Alaskan adventure was about to begin and I was ready.

My mind returns to the present as I walk up the path carrying my fly rod and net, eagerly anticipating all that the day might bring. Tall grasses brush against my hand as a slight breeze moves the dull yellow reeds in a rhythm; they seem to be motioning me forward, and I move in response. Rounding the corner, I begin to hear the rushing waterfalls. The sound intensifies as I progress around a smooth rock face and walked into a sun-filled clearing.

Suddenly, I face an open area containing a two-tier drop in a wide stream surrounded by large, brown boulders placed arbitrarily along the edges of the drop-offs. Large evergreens and other deciduous trees border the stream on both sides, and there are a few large limbs hanging loosely over the water, which threaten to topple in at any moment. Clear water rushes down the stream and crashes over the two combined waterfalls within 100 feet of my position on the hillside. The water churns and forms eddies at the base of the bottom falls, capturing a fallen leaf in an endless whirlpool.

As my eyes drift to the right, I pick up movement at the edge of the woods on the far side. A form begins to appear and I realize it is a large brown bear, its fur tinted on the ends like sun-bleached straw. Quietly and deliberately it moves up the stream while staring down into the swift water, watching for salmon on the way to their final destiny.

Then, out of the deep woods appears another bear slightly smaller than the first, but obviously hungry because of its constant focus on the stream and its swimming occupants. Both bears begin to move quickly toward the rushing water churning over the falls; I slip behind a large tree in order to safely observe them.

Out of the corner of my left eye, I notice more movement. Large, beautifully colored salmon are trying to jump from one level of the water to the next. They leap into the air and hang motionless for an instant, only to fall into the lower pool for another attempt. They are awesome creatures and their varied colors are enhanced by the sun reflecting off their scales, which causes a rainbow effect.

The large grizzlies head directly for the jumping salmon; I remain unnoticed on the far bank. They position themselves on the first drop-off and attempt to grab the fish as they jump and hang momentarily in the air. Eagerly, the bears lean toward the fish, snapping their jaws in the air and catching their prey. Instantly, the sharp and powerful claws seize the slick flesh and the fish is torn apart by the bear's teeth. The white outer skin of the fish is pulled aside in long strips and the raw orange meat is exposed as the body continues to jerk from side to side.

The other salmon appear oblivious to the carnage around them as they jump and reach the upper level in a rush. Successfully entering the strong water above the top of the falls, they give a quick flip of their tails and disappear in the current, pulled upstream by some unknown source toward their final mating ritual.

The bears eventually finish their evening meal and exit the stream. I catch a last glimpse of both as they wander into the maze of trees on the far bank and disappear. With my unused fly rod in my hand, I move away from my hiding spot and work my way back toward the path. I have caught more than fish on this outing in the wilderness; I have witnessed nature in a form not seen by most outdoorsmen in a lifetime.

My memories are very vivid about this particular day, and they add a deeper meaning to my life as a whole. I am truly thankful for them and the comfort they give me.

ALASKA MEMORIES
Ed Hearn

All I have to do is close my eyes and I can drift away to a wonderful place full of adventure and excitement.

As the long ago scene slowly forms in my mind, I am standing on the edge of a remote and isolated stream in the wilds of Alaska. My senses are filled with the soft sounds of running, crystal clear water along with the sight of bright sunshine and azure blue skies, spotted with small white clouds on the horizon. The wind is blowing gently through the tall yellow grass, which is growing profusely along the banks of the stream and the bordering woods that surround me. Everywhere is the virgin smell of untouched wildness with small bits of the familiar.

Have I been here before? Yes, about twenty years ago, but the site hasn't changed and my inner self can still reach out and touch its uniqueness. As I again float back in time, my mind gets even clearer about the memories.

I am now standing with a long, bamboo fly rod in my right hand with the dark green line, connected to a brightly colored fly with its barbed hook in my left hand. As I raise the rod tip toward the heavens to get a long cast, I realize the white-tipped ripples on the surface contain the dark, flowing fin tips of Sockeye Salmon moving carefully up the stream. They move in a thick mass, which covers fully half of the width of the stream flowing by my wading boots. They seem to be winding up the current like a snake slipping up on its prey, totally unaware and unconcerned that I am temporarily entering their world of solitude.

My first cast of the artificial fly lands on the surface and quickly sinks through the movement and into the flow of sleek flesh traveling toward their ultimate fate. A sharp tug on my line brings back a rush of adrenaline, which propels me to action. The battle is instantly on and neither of us is sure of the ultimate outcome. For the ill-fated salmon it is the possibility of escape and survival for a few more weeks, and for me it is the possible satisfaction of conquering one more of life's challenges and becoming the winner in this test.

As I pull back on the rod tip, my friend on the line breaks the surface and catches a glimpse of his adversary. As if in slow motion, he stands on his tail and slides over the surface in an attempt to tease me. His size is impressive and the iridescent colors glisten in the sun as the moisture runs down his side. We are both instantly determined to continue this dance to its conclusion.

About the time I begin to feel in control, I realize I am losing. Line is stripped through my left hand as the fish makes a long run up the stream. All I can do is hang on and wait for him to turn or slow down in the powerful waters.

Just as the last of my line is pulled from the reel, the salmon seemingly hears me pleading. I am able to regain some of my connection as I walk toward him and reel in the line at the same time. He then quickly parts the surface and smiles at me one more time before disappearing into his underwater world. The line goes slack and I know he has won.

While standing quietly in a brief moment of silence, I reflect on what has just happened. I have suffered defeat, but I really don't care. The realization that there can be complete victory in the struggle, floods through my mind. I know now that we both have won and a veil of contentment sweeps over me.

As I lift my head and look toward the skies to take a deep breath, I see two eagles diving from the heavens in a mating ritual. They are tangled with grasping talons and tumbling over and over toward the earth while only breaking apart before hitting the treetops.

I slowly lean over and pick up the rest of my gear from the ground and start back down the narrow path toward the floatplane, which is to take me back to the lodge for the night. My mind is quiet and my soul is at rest. With satisfaction, I realize that I am happy.

MAGICAL CHRISTMAS
Ed Hearn

My family didn't have a lot of extra money when I was young, but that really didn't affect the magical quality of Christmas in the year of 1954. I was only five-and-a-half-years old at the time; my younger brother was four and my older brother was a little over nine years old. We lived in a small block home that Dad and Mom had built with their own hands. The inside of the home included one large main room with two blocked off bedrooms to one side, a very small kitchen and a single bathroom.

Dad and Mom had decorated a small tree in the main room and filled it with colorful, bright bubble lights plus plenty of silver tinsel and angel hair. Each day I had visions of Santa Claus coming on Christmas Eve and bringing me a lot of special toys.

The days seemed to drag by and each night all three of us children would climb into the big bed and let Dad tell us stories about Christmas. During the rest of the year he would be full of nightly tales he made up about Captain Scuttlebutt, but Christmas was very special and during this time he got into adventures about the reindeer, the North Pole, the elves and so forth. Dad's mind was very creative in that way and we enjoyed every story.

Finally, it was the night before Christmas. We three kids jumped into our big bed in one of the bedrooms and begged Dad to come and start retelling his Christmas stories. We were excited and it was the only way to pass time. Dad retold every story he could remember and each time he changed the story, we straightened him out with how he had told it to us the first time. We always looked forward to Dad's storytelling as an important time in our family. After about an hour of listening, we finally got tired and dad slipped out of bed to go to his bedroom as he noticed all of us were breathing heavily with our eyes closed.

On this particular night, I was so excited that I could not stay asleep and woke up a few hours later. I bumped my younger brother so he would wake up and told him that I planned to stay awake to get a peek at Santa Claus when he came to our house during the night. My younger brother said that he was tired but that he would try to stay awake. We lay in the bed for what seemed like hours staring at the ceiling and giggling about it being the night before Christmas. All this time my older brother was sleeping soundly on the far side of the bed and didn't move at all.

I finally decided that I needed to go to the bathroom so I slowly got out of bed and tiptoed toward the small bathroom. My younger brother was falling in and out of sleep and I didn't think he could hang on much longer. I headed directly to the bathroom and on my return trip to the bedroom; I glanced toward the dark area in front of me, which contained the Christmas tree. All the lights were turned off but in the moonlight I could see there were many wrapped gifts under the tree. How had they gotten there since I was awake most of the night?

Just as I was about to go forward and get a closer look at the presents, I noticed what looked like a person standing off to the left of the tree. Could it be true? Was Santa still in the house and had not yet finished delivering our gifts? All I could see in the dark room was a red suit and a short guy with a white beard. He wasn't moving and it scared me. I ran to the bedroom and jumped back into the bed.

I had to wake up my younger brother again.

I told him, "You are not going to believe this but Santa Claus is in the living room right now delivering our toys and presents. I just saw him."

I believe my brother was so tired that he really didn't care but for me I could hardly stay still. Just as I was about to get back out of the bed and take another peek around the corner, one of the stories dad had told us came to mind. It was the story that explained that if you ever saw Santa while he was delivering your toys, he would not leave them and would go on to the next house. I had instant fear about my encounter a few moments earlier in the larger room. What if Santa had seen me and was planning to take everything I saw under the tree with him? What a horrible thought.

I lay completely still and tried not to move. The minutes passed very slowly and all I could think about was to question in my mind if the toys were still under the tree. There was not one sound in the house but I figured that Santa had some method to keep everything quiet so he could unload all his boxes and presents without waking anyone.

Had he already left?

About this time I could tell there was a little morning light coming through the window to the side of the bed. This was great because I couldn't stand it much longer. I lay still for about another fifteen minutes and then pushed my younger brother awake. I told him it was Christmas morning and again relayed the story about seeing Santa in the next room with the tree during the night.

My brother asked if Santa was still there and I said that I didn't know. We both eased out of bed at the same time and crept toward the bedroom doorway together. We peeped around the corner in hopes that Santa was now gone and the presents were still under the tree. Sure enough, the presents were still there and they were everywhere. They were wrapped with colorful paper in many bright colors with bows and ribbons on each package. We had hit pay dirt.

Then, to the side of the tree we noticed Santa Claus. Oh no!

We walked up closer to him since we knew we had already messed up. He wasn't moving and definitely not saying anything. I reached out to touch him and discovered that it was a life-size color image of Santa mounted on heavy board and standing up against the wall. Suddenly, I was relieved, but my younger brother couldn't have cared less. He was on the floor and tearing into the presents and the first one he opened was a can of dog food. Dad and mom had wrapped a gift for our puppy and my brother found it first. That one was discarded quickly and the next present was torn open. He had no desire to only open his gifts and was opening everything in sight. Boy, what a Christmas! This was great!

Dad, Mom and my older brother entered the room and got in on the action. Dad started handing us our individual gifts and the present opening was furious. My older brother got his first BB gun air rifle and my younger brother and I each got a little red wagon. My older brother got a red cowboy hat and my younger brother and I got a matching set of six shooters. There was a standing chalkboard with colored chalk and a bunch of toy cars and trucks. I can't remember all the other gifts but this was surely one special Christmas. We played on the floor for hours and finally Dad and Mom started cleaning up the mess of ribbons and colored wrapping paper. We ate a late breakfast and I began to tell my story of seeing Santa during the night.

I told dad exactly what had happened and how afraid I was that Santa might take the toys with him since I had actually seen him. Dad started to laugh loudly. We all looked across the room and sure enough, the cardboard Santa would fool anyone.

Dad explained how he had been given the mounted, life-size Santa at his workplace. The Coca-Cola salesman had a few extra of them in his truck when he stopped by a few days earlier, since they had been used for advertisement around town to promote the drink. As I looked at the Santa in our house, he actually was holding a Coke in his right hand, which I had never noticed. Dad laughed and laughed.

Many Christmas mornings came and went in the following years, but none were quite as special or remembered for as long as this one.

THERE REALLY IS A SANTA CLAUS
Ed Hearn

On the Christmas Eve of 1956, I still very much believed in Santa Claus.

My brothers and I had made our lists of things we wanted to receive that Christmas; generally, they were items either advertised on TV commercials or shown in the Sears catalog. For days in advance, we looked through the Sears catalog and wrote down different toys we wanted Santa to bring us. As we turned in our lists to Mom, we really didn't know which items Santa might bring.

The air was energized with excitement after the sun went down and I couldn't keep still. Mom realized my brothers and I needed to be distracted and had asked my younger brother and me to follow her into the back bedroom so she could read *The Night Before Christmas* from a well-worn book with colorful pictures.

As she was finishing, we heard, "Merry Christmas! Merry Christmas! Ho, Ho, Ho!"

Completely taken by surprise, my brother and I jumped off the bed and ran down the hallway to the living room, where we heard the front door slam hard. We immediately rushed into the main area to find the base of our live Christmas tree entirely covered with wrapped presents that had not been there before. There were many gifts of varying sizes wrapped in red, blue, green and white Christmas paper, stacked randomly under the tree, which exposed bows and ribbons for decoration on the packages under the lights on the tree. How had they all appeared so suddenly?

Dad and my older brother were standing to the side of the room as we entered and Dad said, "Santa Claus just left through the front door in a hurry and he was the one you heard."

Quickly, my younger brother and I rushed outside the house but didn't see anyone in the dark. We ran back inside and demanded to know, "Why didn't you come and get us while he was still here?"

We dropped down to our knees on the floor and started searching for the presents that had our names on them. As we tore into the many individual gifts, our uncle and aunt knocked on the front door. When they entered, I told them, by almost yelling, "You just missed seeing Santa Claus!" My uncle laughed and laughed as he and my aunt sat to watch the fun.

Years later I found out that my uncle, who had no children at the time, wrapped all our presents and stored them at his house across town. He then brought them over while Mom was reading the Christmas story to us in the back bedroom. My uncle, dad and older brother had taken the presents out of his car and put them all under the tree. He was the one who had yelled, "Merry Christmas! Merry Christmas! Ho, Ho, Ho!"

Their surprise for us that night had worked perfectly and created a lasting memory of a wonderful Christmas. By the time the next Christmas arrived, I had been told the truth about Santa Claus and it was never the same. Now, all those memories flood through my mind–the good times and the bad times. I am thankful for all of it and proud that I have made it to this point in my life so I can share the many stories from the past with my children and grandchildren.

Even now, I can still close my eyes and easily drift back to that night in 1956 and remember vividly what it was like to be a seven-year-old boy who truly believed in Santa Claus.

A MORNING OF ENLIGHTENMENT
Ed Hearn

I've found the quiet time of the morning to be a good time to search my soul and explore my inner feelings. One particular morning when I was twelve, my thoughts turned to the question, "What if I could do it all over again?" What if I could start my life over and make new, fresh decisions about what I did with each of those days of the past?

How many of us have thought about that as we have traveled through life and had to live long-term with our constant decisions to be made every day? I've heard numerous people over the years say, "If I had it all to do over again, I would make the same decisions." From others I've heard, "I would definitely make different decisions if I could have that opportunity again."

Any way you look at it, we are where we are in life because of where we live, what we think daily, how focused we are about the direction we are headed and how pulled we are in directions by others around us who we care about. I think you also have to consider a little "luck" in that equation and maybe the fact those things are meant to be as they are for a reason or purpose. Each time we face that major "Y" in the road ahead of us, we have to make a decision and from there, everything changes.

When thinking along these lines, I usually go back in my memory to a time when I was twelve years old. One warm, sunny day I was bored and had stretched out on a park bench under a large, shady hackberry tree. As I looked up through the thousands of green leaves almost blocking the sunshine and smelled the freshness in the air, I took in the magic of the moment. My mind began to wander. The focus was on time and where I was in my life. At age twelve, I had everything still in front of me. I could direct my life in a way to affect many people in a positive way. Did I really want this? The mindset hit me that maybe I had already lived my entire life in the past and everything had gone wrong. I had made a lot of bad decisions that hurt a lot of people, including me. Maybe I could now be given a second chance. If I started right now, I could do it all over and be given that option and realization. I don't personally believe in reincarnation, but these thoughts were in that direction. Maybe I was realizing that now was the time to start making my life something truly special.

In an instant, on that park bench, I decided to focus regularly on each of my remaining days in an effort to make the most of my life and be a positive influence on many other people. Immediately, I began to study harder each day to make the best grades possible in school. The decision was also made to become involved in athletics while in high school and give it my best effort.

As the years went by afterward, I achieved great things in both those areas, including later on in the business world, art world and relationships with friends. At this time I'm very proud I had that vision on the park bench that turned my life and daily focus around at the age of twelve. In that moment many years ago, I had decided to make my life "the best it could be." I didn't realize at the time how hard that can become sometimes.

After thinking about this personal experience and the effect it had on me throughout my life, my thoughts carried forward to a more current memory of value. Last fall I went to visit a very good, longtime friend who was dying of cancer. He knew he didn't have long to live but at the time was not in any great pain.

We sat quietly together as I asked him about his life and his view of death. His response was simple. He told me that he had lived a good life with a lot of successes. As a gifted artist, I knew he had created a mass of beautiful art pieces of sculpture just in the time I had known him. He had owned a successful business for many years, which he sold for a lot of money in order to retire.

The most interesting part of the conversation on that day was when he said that he was ready to die. His sickness had evolved over almost two years and he had gone through numerous trips to the hospital for chemotherapy. At that time he was weak and tired but his attitude was still positive. When I left him that day, I actually thought he was beginning to do better and might be able to hang on for quite a while. I was wrong. He died just two weeks later; about three days before Thanksgiving.

As I think back about him now, I'm glad he and I had that conversation because it put us both more at peace. He was able to see that a close friend still cared about him and I gained valuable insight into the process of dying. He had told me as we left each other for the last time, "I wouldn't have done anything different in my life. I've had a great life."

It's my hope that one day we will all be able to speak those same final words.

A LIFE-CHANGING STRUGGLE TO SURVIVE
Ed Hearn

I'm alive and I know this is where I have lived all my life. The warm, clear waters of central Florida surround me and offer a perfect place to daily explore and catch small crawfish, worms and other unsuspecting minnows for my food. I've known for some time that I have it good. Everywhere that I look there are large areas of loose grasses and reeds through which I can navigate with great ease. This skill has been developed over many years of my moving cautiously through this liquid space. I am a hunter to be feared and there is this internal sense that I control my own destiny here in my world.

Back when I was growing up in the lake as a young female bass, I had to fight more frequently for the place I wanted to live and hunt for the best food. Frequently I was chased and pushed by others from where I wanted to be. I always knew that one day I would be considered the best and everyone would respect my wisdom and strength. Now I choose where I want to live and the large reed bed of cattails offers a spot of envy to all the others that I rule over. I allow no others of my type to approach this area without an aggressive reaction from me.

Today is like all the others, except I know the time has come. The roe inside me have to be deposited in the bed I have made at the edge of the reeds. Slowly over the last few weeks I have grown fatter and slower in anticipation of this moment. The time has finally arrived.

My smaller mate challenges me to enter the depressed hole in the sand and puts on a display that is unnecessary. I am ready and his efforts are to please himself. As I settle in the nest and press against the bottom, the roe begins to flow from me with a warm sensation. All I feel is relief. The pain is small considering how uncomfortable I have been for weeks as I have waited for this moment. As I move away from the egg laying, my mate moves into the area to deposit his sperm over them with care. I am proud. The job is done and I feel much better. All that fills me now is a motivation to remain over the eggs and fan them with my side fins to keep them clean and healthy.

Off in the distance I can hear another one of those objects moving across the surface. It seems to be approaching my territory. All that comes to mind is to remain still and be cautious. It will pass like all the others over many years. Behind the flat bottom showing through from the surface above me is a churning device that cuts the water and seems to propel it forward. Closer it comes and finally it is silent. I wait and continue to guard my precious clutch as my mate brushes me aside so he can fan the eggs and give me some rest.

As I move to the side, it becomes obvious to me that I have not eaten in a long time. My hunger is intense and I begin to consider moving through the area to see if there is an easy meal lurking nearby. I begin to hear noises and voices from above but I have heard these before. I'm not concerned. I am too smart for these hindrances to interfere with my activities. All I can think of is the incredible pains of hunger that are now pushing me forward and away from the reeds where I feel most safe.

The noise from above has dimmed and my world is again normal. There are no other creatures moving in the sand and smaller reeds around the outer edges of my home. Farther away where the light is not as bright, I can see small minnows darting back and forth but they are too small to be worth the effort. I'm looking for something bigger because I know that's what it will take to rid me of the hunger pains on this day.

Suddenly, there is hope. Appearing on the surface is a large fish that seems to be restrained in some way. Can this be true? This is too easy. I have learned that if something is too easy, there is usually a reason to exert caution. Slowly, I move toward the surface and my desire to eat is intense. This smaller fish seems to be about seven inches long and healthy enough. What is wrong with it; why can't it swim away from me as usual?

Dismissing my fears, I move forward with all the speed I have and grab the fish in my mouth. Something is not right because it is quickly jerked from me and I see it again near the surface in the brighter water. This meal will not be taken from me. With all the strength I can muster I move up and over the meal and engulf it as I roll and head back toward the reed bed. I have fed and I'm headed home to check on the little ones.

Just as I approach the edge of the mound, my head is jerked backward with a force I have never experienced. There is a sharp pain in my jaw and I spit out the meal I have just swallowed. Something is seriously wrong and I can't figure it out. My instinct tells me to run. My efforts carry me to the far end of the weeds and I leap toward the surface in an effort to rid myself of the hurt in my head. As I leave the water and lift into the air, I see the source of my problem. Fishermen are in a boat not far away and they are screaming and waving. My fears increase and I realize that I am in a fight for my life. My best course of action is to continue fighting and jumping in an effort to throw the hook, which is now embedded in my tough skin. My thoughts go quickly back to the eggs that I have just laid on the bottom and whether they will survive if I cannot return to guard and fan them. I must escape or I know they will not make it.

Back and forth I race with all the strength inside me. I know that if I can lift into the sky above and give one more shake of my head, the hook will surely fly from my mouth. In the air I shake like crazy. It isn't working. Back into the water I return and I now realize I am tiring quickly. I'm being pulled toward the object on the surface where the fishermen continue to scream and wave their hands. Just as I reach the surface and near their boat, I make one last rush and show of strength. Heading toward the bottom with all the strength left in me, I am suddenly blocked by an interwoven wall of cords. I'm being lifted upward against my wishes. My heart is pounding and I'm exhausted. All is lost and I realize that I have now been caught by a foe that is stronger and more powerful than me.

There are shouts of joy from within the surface object. I see them patting each other on the back like they have really done something incredible. How foolish are these creatures? Don't they know what they have done? My babies far below in the nest will never survive without me at their side.

I now hear one of them saying, "Weigh that sucker. It must be at least ten pounds."

The next thing I know, I am being lifted by my lip and my entire body is hanging and supported by only that spot. Total pain, but I know it's over for me and all I can do is relax.

One of the other figures standing near me now exclaims, "She's over twelve pounds. I think about twelve pounds and one ounce according to these scales. Let's measure her."

All I can think of at this moment is how badly I need to breathe. Since I am no longer surrounded by the liquid I am used to, my lungs are beginning to ache. I feel a tape being run down my side and everyone stands even closer to get a look. My thoughts are for them to please hurry because everything is beginning to blur from my lack of oxygen.

Again I hear voices and a reading of the measuring tape, "She's 29 and ¾ inches in length. Man, that's the biggest bass that I've ever seen."

How disgusting. Don't they know how crazy they are acting? Please just let me go back to my eggs that need my care and attention. I now feel a pressure around my belly. The fools are measuring my girth. What are they up to now?

The measurement is read out loud to my amazement. The big guy who pulled me into the boat shouts with excitement, "Eighteen inches! She is a full eighteen inches around the girth. That's massive."

I see out of the corner of my eye one of the others grabbing a device he calls a camera. I'm being held up in the air by my strained lip with all my weight dangling for a stupid picture. Not just one. Not just two, but many times they snap photos of me in my misery. When will this end? Have they not had enough yet?

The world is getting dimmer and dimmer for me. I know that I will not make it much longer. The surface of my skin is beginning to dry out and my scales are beginning to rise into the air. Please put me out of my pain. Quit acting like such fools.

Just as I am about to give up, I feel the cool water surrounding my body on all sides. I am being lowered into my world but I am too tired and exhausted to move. Gently, I am being moved back and forth through the liquid and my lungs are beginning to fill with oxygen. I can now breathe. What will happen next?

I hear from above, "We had better let her go. I don't want this one to die. There are not many of this size and I want to have the opportunity to catch her again at some future date."

What a foolish statement. Do these nuts think I will ever allow this to happen again if I can get away this time? Suddenly and without warning, I am released. At first I don't move. I'm not sure what's about to happen, but I advance with caution. With one quick flick of my tail I am again in the darker depths of the familiar water and near the reeds where I feel safe. I advance toward the nest and notice the male is still busy fanning my little ones.

Over me I can hear the start of an engine as the flat object on the surface moves away. There is still shouting and laughing coming from that boat as the fools continue to celebrate. All I can feel is relief. My world is again returning to normal and my energy is returning. There is still a hurt in my jaw but I can live with that until it gets better. I now know that my babies will survive and that is all that matters. Again, I am at peace.

A FOURTH OF JULY TO REMEMBER
Ed Hearn

Suddenly, there were big, loud explosions, bright white lights in every direction and smoke filling the air all around us. We dove to the dew-covered ground and covered our heads with our hands. *What was happening?* Lying on the ground with my younger brother beside me, I was filled with fear and prayed that this would soon be over.

At first I didn't know exactly what had happened, but then I pieced it together. The small firecracker with its fuse burning brightly must have landed in the brown grocery bag standing open beside us. I had lit the firecracker fuse with a hot, burning sparkler and when it burned my fingers, I had immediately dropped it…directly into the fireworks bag. That bag had been filled with individual "black cats," lady fingers, cherry bombs, M80s, whistlers and bottle rockets - all piled on top of each other.

It seemed as if all of them had exploded at the same time. The paper bag was blown into pieces three feet away and the individual firecrackers jumped in all directions as they exploded. The rockets took off through the air while making loud noises, leaving bright streaks of light in the darkness. Most of the bigger and more powerful fireworks simply exploded beside us and shook the ground.

My brother (age twelve) and I (age fourteen) had decided earlier that day that once it got dark, we would try to rid our yard of a groundhog that had recently taken up residence not thirty feet from our small house. Tossing a few high explosives into his fresh burrow would surely scare him to a more favorable location farther away.

We had been able to pitch a couple of powerful cherry bombs and three M80s in the hole before our accident occurred. On that moonlit night we never knew if he had been home in the burrow when the fireworks show went off, but we never saw him again after that evening. It must have been something special for him to experience from his perspective and I'm sure he got a laugh out of our folly.

Now, whenever we are together and the subject of the Fourth of July comes up, we always laugh about that explosive night so many years ago.

Memories…they're what we carry forward, and hopefully, we retain the positive ones.

FISHING THE EASY WAY WITH EXPLOSIVES
Ed Hearn

This story took place when my brother and I were approximately twelve and fourteen years old; I still laugh when it comes to mind.

Dad loved to come home in the early spring afternoons after work and do a little crappie fishing off our boat dock in the backyard. We lived on the shore of a nice freshwater lake in Tennessee. He would go to a lot of trouble to "bait" the dock area some months earlier in preparation of the short crappie season, which only lasted from late spring into early summer. Before New Year's Day, he would use our flatbed trailer to gather about fifteen used Christmas trees that were discarded along the roadside in the neighborhood. The trees would then be weighted down in the water with old concrete blocks and spread all around the three outer edges of our dock. This provided the fish a place to breed and gather in the early spring so they could be easily caught.

The water around our dock was anywhere from eight to ten feet deep along the outer fringe and about five feet deep on the two sides. The bottom of the lake would be completely covered with the trees within this area when dad finished placing them in preparation of the fishing season. He usually tested this baited area each night after work with a minnow, hook and float on a long cane pole that was left lying on the dock for that purpose. When the fish began to bite in the spring, Dad could hardly wait to arrive home from work so he could have some fun.

My brother and I were usually able to fish after school for a while before Dad arrived home from work. On one early spring day, we realized that we had saved a few cherry bombs from the Christmas vacation celebration. At that time, these fireworks were very powerful. We wondered what would happen if we dropped a cherry bomb in the water and let it explode.

We laid ten to twelve of these explosives on the three outer sides of the dock and then lit two separate cigarettes in order to easily be able to light the fuses as fast as we could.

Starting on opposite sides of the dock, we lit one fuse right after the other. As each fuse was lit, the explosive was pushed off the dock into the water where it fell to the bottom of the lake. They were waterproof and the water would not extinguish them. The fuses all burned slowly and gave us time to be off the dock before the cherry bombs started exploding underwater.

We didn't have to wait long. Before we knew it, there were crappies floating on all three sides of the dock. This was a big surprise to both of us. The fish floated to the surface and were quivering because the separate explosions had temporarily stunned them. Using a big dip net, we began to scoop all the fish up as fast as we could before they recovered. They were all put into a big metal wire fish basket in the water which began to fill quickly. There must have been at least forty really nice crappies in the basket when we finished. They began to turn upright and swim after a few minutes as they recovered from the explosions. We stepped back and looked at the metal wire basket and decided dad would be really proud of us for catching all of these fish. At this time it was still an hour before he was to arrive home.

Later in the evening, Dad arrived and was excited about getting to fish after a hard day at work. He quickly asked, "Are the fish biting?" My brother and I just looked at each other and decided to play a little joke on him.

My brother said, "Go down to the dock and see for yourself what's in the basket in the water."

The next thing we knew, Dad was fishing like crazy on the edge of the dock after viewing the contents of the fish basket. He must have stayed there trying every method he could come up with for at least two hours. He didn't get a bite. I watched him from the back porch of our house and saw him go over and repeatedly stare into the basket in amazement. He couldn't figure it out and I knew this by the way he was shaking his head from side to side while looking down into the basket full of large crappies. By this time, my brother and I knew we were in trouble if we told the truth.

Dad finally gave up and came up to the house and asked the big question: "How did you catch so many fish when I can't even get a bite?"

Do you think we told Dad? No. Not for many years. One day about thirty years later while we were all sitting around at one of the family get-togethers, the story came up. At that time we finally told dad what had actually happened and he responded by just laughing out loud. He said that he never could figure out how we caught so many fish and he couldn't get a bite.

We surely had some interesting fishing experiences as a family over the years and it was a wonderful way to spend time with our dad. I think back and it seems like we must have gone fishing with dad over a few hundred times and an interesting story can be remembered about each of those wonderful outings.

FISHING TRIP TO FLORIDA FOR BIG BASS
Ed Hearn

My older brother and I traveled to the middle part of Florida in the spring a few years ago and hired a professional guide to take us bass fishing. This fishing guide told us immediately upon arrival that we should have been there the week before, since his two clients had caught two very big bass and both were in the neighborhood of eleven to twelve pounds. This information got us really excited so we could hardly wait to get started on our fishing trip with him.

As we traveled across the lake to the first fishing location, we passed another guide and two men in a separate fishing boat. We slowed as we pulled alongside of their boat to ask if they had caught any large bass.

The man simply remarked, "Look behind us in the water on the line trailing our boat."

As they eased by us, we noticed they were pulling a long stringer containing two bass larger than ten pounds each; both men looked very excited. They quickly explained that they were from Illinois and were really glad to have already caught two trophy bass that were large enough to mount on their office walls.

Later that same day, we passed them again on the far side of the lake and their moods were entirely different. They explained that after we had first seen them, a big alligator had come to the surface behind their boat and grabbed both trophy fish on the stringer in the water. All that they currently had left were the heads of those large bass. They were both sick about the outcome, but it just excited my brother and I more since we knew we were sure to catch a big one for ourselves.

Our guide then took us to his favorite spot on the lake and showed us a few of his tricks about how to catch a big bass by using large baitfish, called shiner minnows, which are approximately seven inches long and very active in the water once they are attached to the hook. He had about five dozen of these large minnows in a plastic container for us to use as bait that day. He advised us to stare at the large red floats attached to our lines while they were in the water so we would not miss a quick bite from a big bass.

Suddenly, my float disappeared and I responded with a huge upward yank of my rod to set the hook. I quickly realized that I had missed hooking this fish and it embarrassed me since I had fished most of my life with a lot of success. The guide looked over at me with disgust on his face and exclaimed, "You jerked the rod too hard and probably ripped the hook clear through his lip."

Shortly after this, my brother had the same experience. We waited about an hour and then I missed another fish after trying to set the hook with force, since I knew these were big fish. The guide had a strange, dry sense of humor and slowly reached over to start the motor without saying anything.

My brother said to him, "Where are you going? The fish are still biting."

The guide started the motor, began to move to another place with an odd smirk on his face and said, "Heck, you guys have already hair lipped every darn fish in this area. We need to change locations to find a new place where the bass can still be hooked."

The funny thing about his comment was that he was serious. I believe we got on his nerves by the end of the day by not being able to immediately pull one of the big bass into the boat. We were certainly trying very hard and we both made a decision to not jerk as hard so the hook would stay in the mouth of the next large bass.

The next day we got up early and started out across the lake with our guide in search of a big bass. Before leaving the dock, my brother pointed out that I had placed our lunch in the wrong side of the refrigerator overnight, which turned out to be the freezer. On this morning our four peanut butter sandwiches for lunch were frozen harder than a brick. There was nothing we could do, so we loaded them up and decided they would thaw out during the day.

About midday, our guide let us know it was time for lunch and he then realized he had forgotten to bring any sandwiches for himself. He asked me if he could have one of our sandwiches. I handed him one and didn't think anything about it. As he was opening the wrapper to the sandwich, he announced that he was starving. It wasn't long before he was cursing like a sailor.

The guide exclaimed without hesitation, "What in the heck is this? Is it a popsicle?" The peanut butter sandwich was still hard as a rock and he couldn't figure out why.

My brother said while pointing his finger at me, "That dummy over there put the sandwiches in the freezer last night after we made them instead of the regular part of the refrigerator."

The man decided to not eat and just shook his head from side to side. I decided to go ahead and eat mine even though it was frozen, since I was also starving. But before starting to eat, I wanted to clean some of the fish slime off my hands. There was a small bucket in the boat with a little water so I decided to wash my hands. After finishing, I looked up and the guide had this funny smile on his face. I asked him what was going on.

He took great pride in announcing that the bucket I was washing my hands in was his "pee bucket." He said that was the first time he ever had a client wash up for lunch in his "pee bucket."

"Thanks a lot," I said. He now knew he had gotten even for the frozen sandwich offered to him for his lunch.

GETTING TO KNOW A FLORIDA STATE TROOPER
Ed Hearn

On one of our bass fishing trips to Florida with my two brothers, we took my younger brother's brand new van. He had just bought a beautiful new van with large, comfortable captain's chairs in the front. We started our long drive to Florida from middle Tennessee after having worked all day Friday and the three of us were exhausted.

I decided to drive the van first for a few hours. We stopped at McDonalds before we were far out of town where I ate two Big Mac hamburgers to hold me for the trip. That turned out to be the wrong thing to do.

Both of my brothers lay down on a large mattress in the back of the van to try to get some rest while I was driving. That left me sitting in the big, comfortable captain's chair after dark with a full stomach. My eyelids were getting heavy and I should have pulled over. The next thing I knew, we were going through loose gravel on the shoulder of the road and I was dodging the roadside reflectors when I opened my eyes. Both brothers jumped up to find out what was happening as we stopped in a weeded area beside the interstate. As you can imagine, I was quickly replaced as the driver after some tense and angry words.

This first part of the story sets the stage for a later happening on our return trip home.

A few days later, after getting very little sleep while fishing non-stop in Florida, we headed back north on the interstate in the middle of the night. This was done so we could go directly to work the next day on Monday morning.

It was about midnight and my younger brother was driving. I was in the passenger seat and my older brother was lying down in the back on the mattress. He was sunburned so bad his face looked like a lobster. He had told us that he was very tired, and he told my younger brother to definitely not let me drive the van while he was asleep.

We turned on the CB radio. This was during the time in the middle 1970s when everyone had their own two-way car CB radio and talked constantly to the other drivers and truckers traveling on the interstate. All you heard while driving were statements like, "Hey, good buddy," "Put the hammer down" and "There's a Smokey around the corner at mile marker number 75."

My younger brother found someone on the CB who was traveling about two miles ahead of us. That put them in "the front door" position according to CB radio lingo. Then he found someone in "the back door'" position about two miles behind us traveling in the same direction. We determined the location of everyone based on the mile markers posted every mile on the side of the road. My younger brother announced to everyone on the radio that he was in "the rocking chair" since he was in the middle. Both of our other "good buddies" told him he was safe and my brother decided to put the hammer down.

Before we knew it, we were traveling at about 85-90 miles an hour and making good time. My brother was confident of his speed and that we would not be detected because his "good buddies" in front and behind us would let him know if we were near a "Smokey," the name in those days for a state trooper.

Within no more than a few minutes and while traveling at high speed, a flashing blue light appeared behind the van and a voice over a loud speaker told us to pull over. It turned out that by a total coincidence, a state trooper had routinely pulled onto the interstate at the last entrance ramp we had just passed. Since he pulled onto the road right behind us, he could easily determine how fast we were going and we had no notice that he was suddenly behind us. My brother pulled off the road and when the state trooper came up to the van for his driver's license, he asked me to stay seated and then asked my younger brother to come back to his patrol car.

At this time my older brother was still snoring in the back of the van on the mattress. There were two small windows in the van's back doors that allowed the flashing blue lights from the parked patrol car behind us to reflect all around the inside of the otherwise dark van.

You could hear very loudly the state trooper's radio transferring information back and forth to the home office about my younger brother's license. This startled my older brother as he opened his eyes to discover the bright blue lights reflecting and rotating throughout the interior of our van and the police talk coming over the loud speaker. He sat straight up on the mattress and began to quickly feel all over his body in total shock. He looked at me and saw that no one else was in the van.

His first words to me were, "Am I all right?" "Am I hurt? "Have we been in a bad accident?" "Has anyone been killed?" He was terrified.

It wasn't as funny then as it was later on when we thought about it. My older brother was positive, as he woke up, that we had been in a serious accident and he had been knocked unconscious. I have laughed about this story for years and it's a good example of how our fishing trips seemed to go. They were always lots of fun in different ways; something different seemed to happen on each trip.

CATCHING CRAPPIE WITH MY DAD
Ed Hearn

Many times while growing up, my dad would want me to go fishing with him. He loved the outdoors and to be able to go fishing on the weekend was his escape from the pressures of life and a way to relax. It was obvious to me that he was excited about the opportunity to have a good time and he wanted me to be a part of it.

However, these outings involved going fishing with him in the very early morning and getting started before daylight. My immediate thoughts, when asked to go, would be about how tired I would get during and then after the trip, but I would also remember how much fun he would make the entire trip for both of us.

All I had to say was, "Okay, I'll go," and he would take care of all the other details.

Once I agreed to go, he would wake me up about 2:30 AM on Saturday morning since he wanted to get there and start fishing while it was still dark. I would usually stumble out to the car and fall asleep again on the way to a restaurant which was open all night to eat an early breakfast. One of the important things about going on these trips with dad was to stop by a small local restaurant and together eat a good breakfast of eggs, bacon and toast.

We generally arrived at the lake well before the sun started to rise in the sky. Dad would have everything organized in the boat, which included six dozen minnows and two boxes of night crawlers. If the crappie were not immediately biting the minnows, we would then start bottom fishing for large catfish with the slimy night crawlers. As soon as possible we would head out across the open lake, which was as smooth as glass in our small aluminum boat, while I speculated about what we might catch and hope for some big ones. The first hook baited was always the best because if a fish was caught quickly, then we knew the day was going to be a big success.

On one particular trip, dad and I made it to the lake but he was completely exhausted once we anchored down at his chosen spot. We began to fish under two bright, propane lanterns positioned on either side of the small boat and watched the biting mosquitos fly around the lights until he said, "Son, I'm going to take a nap. You go ahead and continue to fish if you want and I will start again in an hour or so after I get a short rest."

After he fell asleep, the crappie began to bite. I was catching two and three fish by using the same minnow, one right after the other, before I had to throw the used bait back and get a fresh one on the hook. I hung our large metal mesh basket over the side of the boat and would drop each crappie in carefully through a trap door so I would not wake dad. The fish were really biting on this night, but they were not very big, only 6-9 inches long were the biggest crappie I was catching. After a couple of hours, Dad began to stir. I was proud of myself and knew he would be excited when he woke up and saw how many I had caught.

Finally, he opened his eyes and said, "Are you still fishing? Have you caught any?"

I was all smiles and proudly leaned over the side of the boat to lift the fish basket so he could see what was inside. The entire basket was filled with so many fish that I could not even open the wire trap door at the top that opened inward. He had to help me lift the basket entirely out of the water because it was so heavy.

Instead of him saying, "Wow, what a good job!" he said, "Oh no! Oh no! Did you not know there is a limit on how many crappie you can legally catch at one time?"

As a young boy, I thought the number you could catch was only regulated by how many would actually fit in the wire basket. Dad then said that we had to do something quickly because the game warden might come along and would surely put us in jail. He started trying to get the fish out of the basket and was having a rough time because they were packed so tightly. There were approximately 100 fish in the basket, to the best of my memory, and that was more than double the legal limit. They were packed so tightly that some of them were already dead.

As Dad dumped them out into the water, many began to float on the surface in an ever-widening circle around us. I looked around and all I could see were dead, white bodies floating on the dark surface. Dad fell over the paddle in his rush to get to the motor to start the engine so we could leave that spot before the game warden showed up.

At the same time, he was saying, "Oh no! Oh no! We need to get out of here quickly."

Once he finally got the boat motor started and we drove off from the area, I recall thinking about how much fun I had catching all those fish and how funny it was that dad reacted that way.

Later on and many times over the years, Dad and I laughed together about that particular trip and other outdoor adventures we experienced. In my mind, I can still see Dad saying, while he shook his head from side to side, "Oh no! Oh no!" Now I think about this story from my youth and it is one of the examples of the good times I had with my dad while growing up, which created positive and lasting memories.

SURPRISING DAD WHILE FISHING
Ed Hearn

My dad and I went fishing together often while I was growing up and on each trip there seemed to be something that happened that was amusing and usually created good memories for both of us.

On this occasion, we were fishing for striped bass. They were not biting immediately so he decided to lie back against the steering wheel of the boat and get a little sleep. I was all fired up and continued to fish after he closed his eyes.

By putting a large hook on the line with a big heavy sinker, I could cast a long distance out into the lake in order to do some serious bottom fishing. My hook was baited completely full with two large night crawlers and I cast it as far out into the darkness as I could. I quickly got a good bite and decided that this was going to be a great fishing trip where I would catch many catfish while Dad slept. He began to snore and I knew he was tired. He had his feet up on the seat and I knew not to bother him.

I was standing at the far end of the boat and time after time the fish would take my bait while leaving only an empty hook. Down to about the last two large night crawlers in the box, I decided to try another place to cast my bait. I figured the farther I threw the hook and weight away from the boat, the better chance I had to catch a large catfish.

Looking at dad I noticed he was really snoring loudly. As I stared out into the lake, all I could imagine was reeling in "the big one." I then stretched back as far as I could with my long fishing rod and heaved the weight and baited hook as far as I could throw it.

Almost instantly I heard a scream behind me and Dad was out of the seat, holding his ear. Glancing at the line, I realized it lead directly to his ear. He looked like he was wearing the metal weight for an earring. I knew I was in trouble. As he took away his hand, I could see that the night crawlers were circling his ear lobe. The hook had completely gone through his ear lobe on the right side of his head and I had snatched him completely out of his seat. I'm still not sure if the weight hit him in the head, but it probably did.

After he settled down and I realized that I wasn't going to get killed for what had happened, we started trying to figure out how to get the hook out of his ear. He had a pair of wire cutters in his tackle box. I got around behind him and cut the barb off the hook while he moaned the entire time. I felt terrible.

My big catfish catch had turned into Dad's ear. I began to laugh, but he didn't think it was funny. I quickly realized it wasn't the thing to do at the moment. Once he recovered from his shock, we fished for about another hour but I believe he was ready to go shortly after the incident because of the pain.

For many years during family get-togethers, we laughed about this unusual fishing trip and it became one of his favorite stories.

There is no wrong or right---Just WRITE!
Right now? Write now!

Dick Nasca was born in Elmira, New York. He is a graduate of Georgetown College and Georgetown Medical School. He completed his internship at the Hospital of the University of Pennsylvania and post graduate training in Surgery and Orthopaedics at Duke and Affiliated Hospitals.

From 1970-1972, he served on the orthopaedic staff at the Philadelphia Naval Hospital caring for Vietnam casualties. He held faculty appointments in orthopaedic surgery at the University of Arkansas School of Medicine and the University of Alabama School of Medicine. Dick specialized in caring for patients with spine deformities, injuries and disorders.

He has been married to Carol T. Smith, RN for fifty years and has three children and one granddaughter.

He volunteers at The Good Shepherd Center for the homeless and as a physician at local medical clinics. Dick has been a member of the University of North Carolina Wilmington Lifelong Learning Program; Advisory Boards at the College of Health and Human Services at UNCW; The New Hanover County Arboretum and Master Gardner Program; Landfall Foundation Board; Landfall Men's Golf Association Board; The Drive, Chip and Putt Program and is a coach with the First Tee of the Cape Fear Region. He has published three books, several book chapters and written seventy peer-reviewed scientific articles.

MY DAY AT PRESTWICK LINKS
Dick Nasca

May 14, 2000 was a bright sunny day in Glasgow, Scotland as I boarded the train for the Prestwick Golf Links. I was dressed to play golf with my golf shoes on and carrying my golf bag over my shoulder when the conductor called out, "All aboard!"

We were underway only a short time when the train came to a stop and our section of the train was separated from the rest of the train. After about a half-hour ride, the conductor approached me and inquired about my final destination as he looked me over in my golf attire. I told him I was going to Prestwick Golf Links.

"Laddy, you are headed to Greenock," he said. "You boarded the wrong section of the train at Glasgow station. You need ot get off at the next stop, cross over the tracks and catch the Prestwick train."

My tee time was 10:30 AM and that time was quickly approaching as I waited for the southbound train.

I arrived at Prestwick around 11:00 AM. To my surprise, the train stop was at the entrance to the golf links. I reported to the club secretary, a middle-aged distinguished looking gentleman dressed in a coat and tie. He informed me that the other three players in my foursome were also delayed and that I was to wait. I took the opportunity to tour the ancient stone clubhouse built in 1851 and to do some putting and chipping.

After a half hour, a young man with a limp summoned me to the secretary's office. The secretary told me that the other three players would not be joining me. He suggested that I go out by myself with Chris, the young caddy who had summoned me. Chris had broken his ankle five months earlier and this was his first trek following four months in plaster.

As we approached the first hole - the Railway hole, a par four - Chris told me to hit a three-iron since anything to the right would find the railroad tracks that paralleled very closely to the first fairway.

On each subsequent hole, Chris explained the design of the hole and where I should place my shots. The fifth hole, called the Himalayas, was a par three of 180 yards fronted by a large crater and laced with sand bunkers. The green was a good 50 feet straight up from the tee box. Chris directed me to hit a five wood that I thought just cleared the front bunker and landed on the green. To our surprise and after much searching, we could not find the ball. I ended up with a triple bogey six on the Himalayas.

Next was Cardinal's Back. This was a short par four with Willie Campbell's Grave, a deep bunker that caused Willie to lose the Open Championship when he took an eight because he was unable to get out of the bunker located about 225 yards out in the center of the fairway. Chris suggested a layup shot, short of Willie's Grave and a mid-iron to the green to avoid the massive Cardinal's Back bunker to the right of the green. For my patience, the Cardinal Back gave me my only birdie of the day. I finished the round shooting a nintey-one.

After we finished, I invited Chris for a beer. Chris told me his brother was an orthopaedic surgeon in Illinois and he was looking forward to visiting him and touring the United States in the coming year. He had caddied at Prestwick for thirty years and had carried the bags of Jack Nicklaus, Lee Trevino and several other great golfers.

The following day after a car trip to Greenock to see my mother-in-law's birth home, my wife and I returned to Prestwick and spent the night at the Old Course Hotel overlooking the fourteenth and eighteenth greens of the Prestwick Golf Links. That evening after dinner we walked the links on a cloudless night full of bright stars and a full moon shining brightly on the Himalayas.

EXIT DELIVERY
Dick Nasca

It was June 25, 1965 - the last of my internship at the Hospital of the University of Pennsylvania. I had packed my car for the trip home to Bethesda, where I would spend a few days before starting my surgery residency at Duke. I had picked up my internship certificate and said good-bye to the intern program director, Dr. Elliot.

As was my custom, I walked through the ER on my way to my car that was parked nearby. As I passed the front desk, Marsha, the head ER nurse, asked me to look in on a young woman who was being brought into cubicle nineteen. She was in active labor with her fourth child.

Marsha lifted her gown and to our surprise we saw a small head of black hair surfacing from the distended perineum. There was no time to do a block and perform an episiotomy. I put on a pair of gloves as Marsha called for a peri kit. Before I got my hands into the gloves, the baby's head was almost all the way out. I guided the shoulders out and the trunk and legs followed. Unfortunately, there were several deep tears that would require suturing.

We tied off and cut the umbilical cord. Peds was called to come to check the baby, whose APGAR was very good. I was instructed to pack off the bleeding and get the mother up to labor and delivery for further care. I had planned to turn the mother over to the OB/Gyn intern for repair of her tears, but he nor the on-call resident were around. The head nurse handed me a scrub suit and told me she would prep the patient.

I was really looking forward to my mini vacation and a few days' visit with my family. As I scrubbed my hands, I reviewed in my mind the upcoming repair of this young woman's multiple lacerations from the precipitous birth of her son. Fortunately, the head nurse had anticipated my need to have an array of instruments, local anesthetics and suture to use.

As I removed the packing, several nasty bleeders started to flood the area. Using suction in one hand and hemostats in the other, I was able to clamp off the major bleeders. I then administered a pudenal block, which gave the patient some much-needed relief.

As I started the repairs, I heard the soft voice of Dr. Payne, chairman emeritus of OB/Gyn over my right shoulder, "Dick, so nice to see you back. Did you take the residency slot at Duke?"

"Yes, I did," I replied. I thanked him for the advice he had given me in October when I got called out of the operating room while assisting him.

It was most unusual for a lowly intern to be called out of the OR for a telephone call. The Chief of Surgery at Duke offered me a surgical residency and I responded to the chief surgeon that I would like to think about his offer. When I returned, Dr. Payne asked me why I had left the OR. I told him I had been offered a surgery residency at Duke. He asked what decision I had given and I recounted my answer. He then instructed me to leave the OR immediately and call the chief surgeon back and accept the position, which I did. Little did I realize then that this would be one of the pivotal decisions of my medical career. I would spend the next five years at Duke, completing a year in general surgery and four years in orthopaedic surgery.

Just as I was finishing the repairs, the intern and resident came in. This was the intern's first day on the service and the resident was showing him around. After removing my scrubs and dressing, I decided to walk out the front doors of the hospital rather than chance another "exit delivery" in the ER.

GRAPES OF WRATH
Dick Nasca

It was a rainy day as my cousin Joe and I started off to school in our yellow rain slickers and rubber galoshes. Joe had lost his mother after his brother Michael was born a year ago. Michael was adopted by their other aunt and Joe came to live with us in Washington, DC.

Joe and I were the same age. He was a prankster, liked to show off and stir up the class when the teacher was out of sight. I was more reserved and less outgoing.

Mom had packed each of us our lunch in brown paper bags. The walk to school was about twenty minutes. As usual, Joe and I played around on the trip to school. After about ten minutes, the skies opened with a big downpour. We sought shelter under the awning of a grocery store on Minnesota Avenue. We had our books and lunch under our slickers, but the wind-driven rain got us soaked.

After about fifteen minutes, the rain let up and the sun came out so we made fast tracks to St. Francis Xavier parochial school on Pennsylvania Avenue. There was no way we could be at school on time. We talked about playing hooky but with Mom and my new sister Geraldine at home, there was really no place to go so we proceeded on to school.

If you were late you had to go to the principal's office and explain why you were late. The principal's secretary recorded our story and gave us a note to have signed by my parents letting them know that we were late for school and that it would not be tolerated. I placed the note in a dry pocket and Joe and I headed for our second grade classroom.

Sister Mary Carol, a sister of Notre Dame, was at the blackboard when we arrived at the classroom door with our wet heads and soaked slickers. In order to keep discipline, each sister was supplied with a six-inch wooden clicker that would provide a command click without the necessity to verbalize. She directed us to the back of the room to hang up our coats and take off our galoshes. As I was headed back down the side aisle of desks, I heard Joe start to laugh and cackle. I was unaware that my paper lunch bag had given way and the green grapes were scattering everywhere along the highly polished floor between the desks of my classmates.

Sister Mary Carol grabbed her wooden clicker off her desk and came running over to me as more grapes exited from under my yellow slicker onto the floor. As each grape fell, she clicked her clicker and pointed it in my direction as a command to pick up each grape. All my classmates were laughing and enjoying seeing me pick up each grape with each click of the clicker. I was mortified and wanted to fall through the floor out of sight.

A few months ago, I attended my sixtieth high school reunion. Five of my St. Francis grade school classmates were at the reunion. My old friend Johnny gave a toast. As he raised his glass of Cabernet, he recalled the "grapes of wrath debacle" that had occurred sixty-nine years ago. Many of us remembered it and we all had a great laugh.

MEETING FORTUNATA
Dick Nasca

Since there were many farms in the small towns around Lercara Friddi, Sicily, many of the farm owners contracted out their work to organizations that employed farm workers. Galogero Latona was the supervisor for the farm management company. He was responsible for hiring the laborers and getting the work done in the fields in a timely fashion.

My grandfather, Nicola, signed on to work as a field hand with Galogero's band of workers. It did not take long before Nicola's skills and work ethic were noticed by the management.

Each day after work, Nicola would report to Galogero on the work he and his crew had done. One day, Fortunata - a young blond girl with blue eyes, was sitting in her father's office as Nicola came in to make his report. After Nicola left, Galogero passed off the information to Fortunata who recorded it in a large, leather-bound journal.

A few weeks later, Nicola was called into the office to meet with Galogero about some of his reports. There was some concern about the numbers of bushels of artichokes that had been recorded by Nicola as picked and the number that had been received by the buyer. Nicola stood by his figures which he had recorded. He was warned by Galogero that if there were any future discrepancies with his numbers, he would be dismissed.

The next day, Nicola stayed late to recount the number of bushels of artichokes picked by his crew. He then followed them into the warehouse where they were to be stored but not recounted by the warehouse manager. It was late in the day but he decided to stay near the warehouse on the hunch that someone was going to remove some of the bushels. Sometime after dark, a wagon pulled up to the back of the warehouse and several bushels were loaded onto the wagon and driven off.

The following day Nicola was called in by Galogero, who told him that his count was again wrong and that he was no longer needed. Nicola then recounted what he had witnessed the previous night at the warehouse. Latona did not believe Nicola. However, he wanted to get at the truth so he told Nicola to go back to work, recount the day's harvest and report to him after work.

When he returned at 5:00 PM, Fortunata was also there. He instructed Nicola to go with Fortunata to the warehouse to recount the bushels. When they got to the warehouse, Nicola and Fortunato did a recount and found that Nicolas' figures reported that afternoon to her father were correct. However, they both noticed that the warehouse manager seemed to be nervous and wanted them out as soon as they did their recount. Rather than leave the area, Nicola and Fortunata stayed around. About an hour later, a wagon pulled up and as before, loaded up several bushels of the artichokes picked by Nicola's crew.

This time Nicola and Fortunata followed the wagon to another warehouse where the bushels were unloaded. A few minutes later, the manager of the previous warehouse appeared and paid off the wagon driver. When Nicola and Fortunata returned to her father's office, Galogero was furious that she was so late in returning and was about to grab Nicola by the neck and strangle him when Fotunata stepped in, put her hand up and said, "Stop!" She then recounted to her father the events that she and Nicola had witnessed at the warehouses.

The next day, Nicola and Galogero went to see Carmine, the owner of the warehouse. He was informed of what had transpired. Carmine, Galogero and Nicola then went to the warehouse. The nervous manager later confessed that he was responsible for the thefts.

A few weeks later, Galogero and Fortunata moved on to another town to supervise another harvest. Nicola stayed in Lercara Friddi to help with the fava bean harvest. In the fall and winter, Nicola kept busy doing repairs on the town streets and buildings. In the spring, he returned to the artichoke fields and vineyards.

MY DAY ON THE OLD COURSE OF ST. ANDREWS
Dick Nasca

In May 2000, I retired, closed my orthopaedic spine practice, and headed to Scotland for a vacation with my wife Carol and daughter Susan. For my sixty-second birthday on May 30th, I was scheduled to play the Old Course at St. Andrews. I had booked the golf session with a Scot living in Fort Worth, Texas who arranged golf trips in Scotland.

We arrived in St. Andrews the afternoon of May 29th and checked into to our hotel. To our dismay, there was one large bed, a rollaway and a small sink in the room with the bathroom and shower at the other end on the fourth floor.

My daughter and I proceeded to the Old Course to check on my tee time and to look the place over. After a few minutes of standing in line at the check in, I handed over my reservation and handicap verification to a dapper-looking Scot. To my dismay, he promptly told me *I had no tee time.* Furthermore, the policy at St. Andrews was to make tee times in advance for foursomes only. Those without tee times desiring to play could be placed in a lottery or just return on the following day around 7:00 AM to wait for an opening.

Since it was past time to be placed in the lottery for May 30th, I returned with Susan to our elegant digs for supper. As we entered the hotel, I ran into the owner who asked how I liked the set-up at St.

Andrews. I told her that I had no tee time and asked if she could assist me with getting one. She told me she had a few lottery slots but had given them out to other guests earlier.

After dinner we walked around the town of St. Andrews and the St. Andrews University. It was still light and we could see students finishing the last few holes at the Old Course, carrying their dark blue bags with the St. Andrews name and logo.

May 30th was a bright and sunny, warm day. After breakfast, I had Susan drive me down to the Old Course. I got my name on the "wait list" and was told to check back around 10:00 AM. I had my clubs and told Susan to go off; I would hit some balls on the range. To my surprise, there was no practice range at the Old Course. I did manage to find a small putting green and an area to do some chipping. At 10:00 AM I sheepishly made my way to "check-in" to face the dapper Scot who had given me the bad news yesterday afternoon.

As expected, nothing had opened up. However, he suggested I stay close and check back in in a few hours. My hopes for a career round at St. Andrews on my birthday were fading fast.

Susan and Carol appeared around 11:00 AM to check on my progress and commiserate with me. I thanked them for coming and told them to return around 1:00 PM. A few minutes later, I ran into a gentleman named Bob from Cincinnati, who was also a single. He had just spoken to a couple who had gotten a tee time and were not pared with anyone else so they had invited him to join them. He spotted the couple and directed me to them. Yes, they would be happy to have me join them.

We all proceeded to the starter's box to sign in. We were told to be ready to play at 12:45 and that I needed to get a caddy. So I hustled down to the caddy house and asked the caddymaster if he had a caddy. He said, "Laddy, I am short but I will see what I can do." We waited as instructed off the first tee for our turn.

Just before I was to tee off, Alistair, my caddy, appeared. Alistair was a former medic and nurse who had taken up caddying at age fifty. Also, Susan and Carol returned to see my opening drive at St. Andrews.

The first hole of the Old Course is as wide as it is long. Alistair instructed me to put the driver away and hit a shot of 200 yards or less with my three wood since he did not want my ball to roll into the "Burn," a channel of water a few yards wide crossing the fairway.

On my second shot, I got across the "Burn" but ended up in back of the green and took three putts for a bogey. I had a score of forty-six on the front nine. I was happy to avoid the pot bunkers and the heavy gorse.

We had some rain showers that lasted a few minutes but really did not cause us any problems. Frank and Gail had their daughter walking with us and she supplied us with candy bars and snacks out of her backpack.

I was really pumped up going to the back nine. On the par five, fourteen-hole called "Long," I made a par. This was rated one of the most difficult holes. I was cruising along nicely; I had not lost a ball or gotten into much trouble in the sand bunkers, some of which are so high and steep you needed to pitch out sideways or backwards.

We came to the famous seventeenth, the "Road" hole. This is a par four of 461 yards. Your blind tee shot has to be hit over a high maintenance shed to a narrow patch of fairway 30-40 yards wide. To the right is the Old Course Hotel and to the left of the narrow fairway, ugly thick gorse and heather.

Alistair lined me up for my blind tee shot over the shed. He indicated that I had positioned it well. However, when we approached the fairway, we could not find my ball. My wife, who was in the courtyard of the Old Course Hotel, saw a ball land in the hotel fountain. She came over with it while Alistair and I were looking for my ball. I took a drop outside the hotel grounds and hit my third shot, which landed on the "Road." Another drop, then my shot to the green. This landed in the bunker to the right of the green. I was happy to end up with a seven on the infamous "Road" hole.

The last hole, number eighteen, is "Tom Morris" with a road across the fairway. The second shot must be long enough to carry the "Valley of Sin." I was fortunate to get on the green in two but took three putts for a bogey. My "Road" hole had done me in. I finished the inward nine in forty-nine for a total score of ninety-five. Considering my fourteen handicap, I shot a net eighty-one.

As I gave Alistair his caddy fee and tip, he put his hand on my shoulder and whispered in my ear, "Doc, you played well but your little wee putter let you down."

We returned to the Old Course Hotel for drinks and dinner. Susan, Carol and I meet up with Frank and Gail and had a few drinks as we reminisced about our round of golf on the Old Course, followed by a great dinner overlooking the "Road" hole.

SHARING THE FOURTH OF JULY
WITH MY ANIMAL CHARGES
Dick Nasca

After my freshman year of medical school, I was offered a summer job with Dr. J.P. in the Physiology Department of the medical school. My assignment was to feed and water the rabbits, guinea pigs and rats used in his iron metabolism study. I also administered into their mouths radioactive iron by syringe. This consisted of holding the animal in a large padded glove in one hand to avoid being bitten or scratched while introducing a long, curve-tipped delivery needle attached to the syringe into their not-so-open mouths.

The long Fourth of July weekend was coming up and I had a full social calendar. The animals were housed in the fifth floor attic of the medical school in less than ideal conditions. I decided to bring the animals to our house for some fresh air and rest on our screened-in side porch. This would also save me from travelling to school to feed and water them over the three-day holiday.

So late Friday afternoon, when all the labs were closed, I brought my caged charges with their food pellets down the freight elevator and loaded them up in my 1952 burgundy, four-door Chevy with rusted floorboards and fenders for a trip to suburbia.

My mother was somewhat concerned when I unloaded the guests onto our porch, but nowhere as surprised as when she opened her basement refrigerator and found a half-dissected cat reeking of formalin that I was working on in undergraduate biology.

On Saturday, I got up early to feed and water the animals before taking off for a pool party and picnic. When I returned in the late afternoon, I noticed that the screen door to the porch was wide open. On further inspection, I saw that several cages were empty and some were missing. We lived across the street from a creek that emptied into the grounds of the National Institute of Health (NIH). We had a huge rain and the creek was swollen with fast moving water.

My younger brother, Ed, convinced my mother that the caged animals really should be freed. You guessed it: Ed and his friends took the animals for a swim in the creek. Several disappeared as the swift current swept them downstream. I searched until dark but was unable to recapture the escapees.

At the break of dawn on Tuesday morning, I loaded up the remaining animals and the empty cages for the trip back to the medical school. As I unloaded the cages from my car, Dr. J.P. pulled up to the medical school parking lot. Needless to say, I had a lot of explaining to do.

Dr. J.P. kept me on in his lab and didn't get me booted out of medical school. Just before I graduated, he called me in to his office and told me that several of the animals had found their way to the NIH and were given asylum there.

TRAIN TO TRUCKEE
Dick Nasca

It was 8:00 AM on a clear cool day in Denver as we waited to board the Amtrak California Zephyr train to Truckee, California for a four-day visit to Lake Tahoe. A few minutes after we arrived, the EMTs pulled up sirens blaring with a stretcher full of resuscitation and monitoring equipment headed to our train on track four. After awhile, we saw the medical examiner board the train with his entourage.

After a long wait, we were instructed to board. We sat for about an hour then we were told that the train would be on its way around 10:00 AM. The train attendants told us that after the car of the deceased was cleaned and loaded with passengers, we would be off. Just before we departed we saw a stretcher loaded with a black bag being pushed down the concourse to the medical examiner's waiting vehicle.

As the train left the Denver station, we went to the dining car to have breakfast. After breakfast we headed for the domed excursion car with the great panoramic views. A retired railroader and another volunteer were in the car to give us an account of how the line was constructed, the grade of ascent and the number of tunnels required to get up and through the mountains of the Continental Divide.

The ascent was gradual, no more than a 2 percent grade. This was accomplished by long stretches of track laid out with narrow hairpin switch-backed curves. You could often see the front of the train on one curve as the rear was on another. There were thirty-one tunnels all blasted out of the granite with dynamite and shored up with wood, stone and cement. At the summit of the Continental Divide lay the longest tunnel of 6.2 miles named for David Moffatt, a Denver banker who financed the initial construction. He wanted to link Denver to Salt Lake City and points west. The line saved 176 miles of travel between Denver and San Francisco. The East portal was near Rollinsville and the West portal opened up in Winter Park Ski Resort. I recall Denver friends talking about day ski trips to Winter Park on the train. The scenery was breathtaking from our rotating seats in the domed car. In addition to the train tunnel there was a parallel 8x8-foot water tunnel that carried Denver's water supply through the mountains.

As we left Granby, we began paralleling the Colorado River, which runs through the Gore Canyon and is only accessible by rail or kayak. The walls of the river ascend some 1,000 feet on each side of the river with several miles of treacherous Class V whitewater. We stopped for a few minutes at Glenwood Springs where the Colorado and Roaring Fork Rivers meet and the Aspen and Snowmass ski resorts are located. As we approached Grand Junction where the Gunnison and Colorado rivers join, we saw the Grand Mesa - one of the world's largest flat-top mountains that ran for miles. The train passed south under I-70 into Utah at 4,000 feet. We had spent the night in Green River a few years ago and had been treated to fresh vegetables, local beef and the best-tasting cantaloupe and honeydew melons.

We caught a beautiful sunset in the western sky as we went through eastern Utah. We had a delightful dinner with an African American couple. He was the CFO of the City of Detroit and told us about how the city was rebounding financially and rebuilding its downtown infrastructure.

After dinner we returned to our seats that had been turned into the lower bed. This was my first experience with a sleeper. After a few attempts, I managed to climb up to the upper pull-out bunk. Whereas the lower compartment had a wide surface of the two coach chairs placed side by side, the upper bunk pull-out was narrow and offered only a few feet of clearance below the train roof, making it difficult to move around. In order to get down from the upper bunk I had to slide down feet-first, hoping to make contact with a foot perch or the lower bunk. I had some trying moments in the dark getting down from my perch to get to the bathroom.

We arrived in Salt Lake City to take on passengers around 1:00 AM, making it difficult to get back to sleep. I was happy when daylight occurred and the dining car opened at 6:00 AM.

We then approached the eastern towns of Nevada: Elko, Winnemucca, Lovelock and Fernley. The scenery was filled with scrub, farms and ranches. As we approached Sparks, Nevada - the twin city of Reno - we saw a number of residential areas and casinos. We made a stop in Reno, "the Biggest Little City in the World," to pick up and unload passengers. Soon we were in California and to our destination in Truckee. We had traveled 1,200 miles, arriving in Truckee twenty-four hours after our departure in Denver.

Our daughter and granddaughter were there to pick us up and take us to our condo in Lake Tahoe with a comfy king-sized bed.

PINK JACKET COVERED WITH BLOOD
Dick Nasca

JFK was shot at 12:30 CDT on Friday, November 22, 1963 as his open car motorcade was rounding the circle of Dealey Plaza in Dallas, Texas. The shots were traced to the Dallas Book Repository overlooking the grassy plaza. Being mortally wounded, the president was taken to Parkland Hospital, a major trauma center close by with Governor John Connally, who sustained gunshot wounds to his chest. Jackie Kennedy was not injured, but her pink suit jacket was covered with her husband's blood as she held him following massive intracranial injury.

JFK was taken from the Parkland emergency room to an operating room where the Parkland surgeons who were on duty that fateful day did everything they could to bring him back, but their efforts were to no avail because of the massive brain trauma inflicted on the President.

JFK's body was flown back to Andrews Air Force Base in Clinton, Maryland. He was transferred from Air Force One into a small navy ambulance for the twenty-mile trip to Bethesda Naval Hospital. Jackie followed in an open car surrounded by secret service cars and a large motorcycle escort. The route from Clinton north onto Pennsylvania Avenue and then through downtown DC, which was lined with people.

My home on Jones Bridge Road was directly across the street from the Naval Hospital. My family had moved to Bethesda in 1951, just a few years after the hospital was completed. My bedroom faced the south tower. My friend Tommy was the son of the commanding officer so I was fortunate as his guest to enjoy the pool, golf course, bowling alley and ball diamonds. My mother worked at the hospital as a bookkeeper for the American Red Cross. My friend Tim's mother Mary was the secretary to the Chief of Pathology who would perform the autopsy on JFK. I had recently been an extern on the Pediatric service at the hospital during my third year in medical school.

I was standing on the corner of Jones Bridge Road and Wisconsin Avenue as the ambulance carrying the President's body made its way north toward the hospital. Jackie was sitting in the back seat of a black Cadillac convertible. As she came by less than thirty yards from where I was standing, I was shocked to see she was still wearing the pink jacket covered with her husband's blood.

For some reason, I decided to walk across the street onto the hospital grounds and into the south entrance of the hospital. There were no guards or security as I entered the first floor. I knew the morgue was in the basement and decided to head in that direction, not really thinking a lot about my decision. As I approached the doors outside the morgue I could hear some voices. I did not dare open the doors into the morgue; I just stood there frozen in time.

A short time later an x-ray tech passed by me with some x-ray cassettes. To my surprise, I got a quick view of the autopsy team surrounding the president's body on the autopsy table as the doors swung open to let the tech in.

My friend Tim's mother typed up the autopsy report on President Kennedy. I had hoped to read it, knowing that she had kept a copy, but she never let anyone see it nor did she ever discuss it. I wonder now, fifty-three years after that historic day, why I was so brazen to go to the morgue and why Jackie had decided not to change her pink jacket covered with blood.

DENVER CHRISTMAS BLIZZARD OF 1982
Dick Nasca

We were driving down to Denver following a week of skiing to spend the night at Stapleton Airport. We had reservations on a flight leaving December 24th for Atlanta and then on to Birmingham, Alabama. We were anxious to get home to celebrate Christmas with my parents, my brother and his wife. We had decorated the Christmas tree and had all the presents wrapped prior to leaving on our ski trip.

The night of December 23rd was very clear with not a cloud in the sky. It was warmer than usual as we approached Denver. Unknown to us, this warm air mass was carrying a lot of moisture from the Gulf. Within a few hours, three major storm fronts would collide over Denver resulting in blizzard conditions.

Three feet of snow fell during the next twenty-four hours with 50-mile-per-hour winds, large snow drifts and a wind chill of -35 degrees. Stapleton was forced to close down at 9:30 AM on December 24th and would remain shut down for the next thirty-three hours.

We were lucky to have a warm room and a place nearby to get food. Many travelers were stranded at the airport. We knew there was no way we were going to make it home for Christmas. We did anticipate that with the weather clearing on Christmas Day we might get out on the December 26th. However, the mayor had given the street crews Christmas Day off so no snow removal was done. Food was getting scarce. Our youngest, Mark, kept asking if Santa was coming. I found out that my dad and mom were alone at our house in Birmingham as my brother and his wife had left for her parents' home in Memphis on Christmas day.

I walked over to the airport on Christmas Day since Frontier Airlines was not answering their phones. There were long lines of people extending in all directions. It became apparent after talking with an agent that we were probably not going to get out of Denver for a least two more days. The runways were piled with snow and there were no plows in sight. The sun came out the day after Christmas as did the snow plows. Unfortunately, there were not enough plows to do the streets and clear the runways so we waited until December 27th.

Another trip to the airport gave us some hope of getting out on a Frontier Airline flight bound for Atlanta. We packed our bags and skis and trudged through the snow over to the airport around noon. Most of the snow had been removed from the runways and a few planes were taking off.

After a few hours we were told that Frontier had a flight scheduled to take off around 7:00 PM for Atlanta. We were lucky to be one of the last to get on that flight. Due to a delay on the runway in Denver, we were late getting into Atlanta and missed the last connecting flight to Birmingham. We camped out in the airport until sunrise and caught the first plane for home.

A few hours after we arrived home, the phone rang. The local TV station was calling to request an interview. Later we found out that our daughter Susan had called the radio station to tell them we were home safely after hearing a reporter talking about the people stranded in the Denver blizzard.

That evening we saw ourselves opening Christmas presents on TV and recounting our Denver Christmas of 1982.

BIRTHDAY SHUTOUT
Dick Nasca

The Second World War was over and I was approaching my eighth birthday on Memorial Day, May 30, 1946. I remember telling my classmates and friends that I was special since I always got out of school on Memorial Day, my birthday.

I had wanted a bike for my seventh birthday but due to the shortage of metal during the war, there were few bicycles being built. Dad had recently picked up a 1938 four-door Chevy sedan and had found parts to refurbish it. He mentioned that maybe he could find me a set of wheels and a bike frame.

My mother always had a birthday party with coconut cake and ice cream and invited all my friends and our neighbors. As soon as I had the cake and ice cream, I was quick to open my presents and then send the guests home so I could enjoy my gifts alone.

My next-door neighbor, Ernie, was older but one of my friends, as was his youngest of four sisters, Gail. Well, Gail was my friend until she hit me across the bridge of my nose with a garden hoe. In any case, I spent a lot of time at Ernie and Gail's house. Ernie's mother Mary was always friendly and had a variety of snacks and cold drinks for us to enjoy.

As my eighth birthday approached, it seemed that no one next door was interested in playing with me and the front door that was usually open was closed. In spite of my repeated rings of the doorbell, no one answered. I finally gave up and then Ernie appeared at my door. He told me I was being a pest and to stop ringing his doorbell. I was really bummed out and told my mother to take Ernie and his sisters off the birthday party list.

At 3:00 PM, the guests and neighbors came all dressed up with their birthday presents in hand. Boy, was I happy that they showed up...and that Ernie and Gail had not. Mother warned me that I was not to get rid of my guests as I had done on previous birthdays.

As the party was winding down, I heard a bell ringing. It wasn't our doorbell; it was another type of bell. I ran out the front door onto our porch and lo and behold, Ernie and his sisters were carrying a shiny red bike up the stairs of my front porch.

I later found out that my dad had found a bike frame and wheels and assembled and painted my new bike. Ernie and his family had hidden the bike behind their living room sofa, which was why I was to be shut out from entry into their house until the bike was delivered to my party.

Start writing, no matter what.
The water doesn't flow until the faucet is turned on.
Louis L'Amour

DIANE TORGERSEN was born in Brooklyn, New York. Her parents moved to Florida, California and then to Oak Ridge, Tennessee during World War II. After the war, they moved to Kingston, Tennessee where Diane lived until graduating from high school. She attended the School of Radiologic Technology in Charlotte, North Carolina.

Diane and her husband and their three sons lived in Texas and Alaska before finally settling down in Maryland. She spent three years in Cheltenham, England, where she attended the Gloucestershire College of Art and Design. Diane remarried and continued studying and working in art and design. They moved to Florida where she continued art classes and began designing art pillows, becoming known as The Pillow Lady. She then moved to Wilmington, NC where she studied abstract painting at UNCW.

Diane has aspired to be a writer since writing essays in the third grade, two of which she still possesses. She always had a "scarlet thread" of writing throughout her life while pursuing other interests and careers. Her signature entry into the writing world began when she joined the Landfall Writers' Group in Wilmington, NC in 2015 where she found a strong voice in writing reflective humor. These stories are mostly drawn from childhood, observations, raising a family and simply living - all done with a commitment to preserving those cherished memories.

FROM ANOTHER GALAXY
Diane Torgerson

Fourth grade was my personal introduction to the mores of the South. Each day I observed changes subtle and not so subtle by simply being among my classmates. Language barriers were the first to sort out - they made different sounds than I did. "Cain't," "ain't," "hain't," "awl" (for oil). They talked with a slower rhythm and somehow managed to add several syllables to a one-syllable word.

They all knew each other like a big family and they nosed up like friendly pups to check you out. The first issue was, "Which side are you on?" I had no idea what they were talking about. "You know," they said, "which side of the Silver War are you on?"

I had never heard of this war. When I asked my dad when I got home, he said, "Just tell them you are from California." That was perfect; that's all they wanted to know. The question never came up again, but I sensed a subtle change in my position among my peers. I was a foreigner.

One of my new friends eventually asked me to ride home on her bus and spend the night. My parents encouraged me to meet new friends, so away I went to what seemed like Never-Never Land. They had no indoor plumbing other than a hand-cranked water pump in the kitchen. That meant using a back house for bathroom needs; not good in the dark.

We roamed through freshly plowed fields while she told me what had been planted; she knew all the little green sprouts. Her mother was kind but busy, having a new baby to care for. To rock the baby to sleep, she sat in a straight-legged wooden chair on a porch with the baby cradled to her shoulder and rocked the chair violently back and forth, causing the wooden legs to slam loudly on the porch. That child was asleep in no time. I now wonder: Was it a mild form of shaken baby syndrome being used as a sleeping aid?

These were the school days in which all subjects were taught in the same room. We only left it for lunch or recess or special programs until we graduated from eighth grade. I loved the lunches, which were only 35 cents. They very often had white whipped potatoes each week, and a dessert. I don't remember any of the desserts, but the potatoes were a marvel of fluffy goodness. Mother's style always had lumps, which I remember affectionately whenever I now run across some in a meal.

I was with this group of people for nine years of my life. We grew from children to young adults together, with all the angsts that go with that. We were like a large group of cousins, knowing where and how to minister goodness or mischief toward each other.

Whenever we now meet at reunions, I am always amazed at the unique ability to be seventeen or eighteen years old again, if only for a few hours. Because that's how we knew each other last.

DANCING WITH THE STARS
Diane Torgersen

Try to imagine what a tiny recorder player sounds like in a school-sized gym. Sitting on the floor, it tries to project its single-song LP melody to the 300 or so students sitting on the bleachers for high school assembly. A tiny sound in a huge space.

Once a week the school asked for students to display their talents for amusement and entertainment - and possibly ridicule - during the early morning program. Some read poetry, some sang . . . once my entire tumbling team supplied a performance with high tosses of each other, arm stands and forward tumbles all in a row. We were a success, probably because we got to wear our bloomer-type gym suits that were bathing-suit short.

This time, however, I was performing solo. I had decided to teach myself dancing. During my sixteen years, I had seen lots of movies featuring dancers: tap, ballroom, ballet. Something in me longed to be a dancer and I decided "freeform" was the ticket. No one could critique it since it had never existed before. It would be my own original.

I saved allowances and bought records that I thought would be appropriate to create scenarios similar to movies featuring Ginger Rogers, Cyd Charise and Leslie Caron and I practiced endless hours.

I made up all sorts of skits that the dancing would fit into and hopefully tell a story. How I managed that solo-style, I have no idea. But they they kept asking me to perform.

Finally, I convinced a couple of my fellow students to dance with me. I designed costumes and made up a story a la Gene Kelly doing the Paris-Apache dance with Cyd Charise. And some foolish boy agreed to do it with me. The school principal even allowed us to use a rather large storage room to practice in when we both had study hall time together. He peeked in regularly to make sure we weren't goofing off and even sat in sometimes while we went thru the paces of generating the story-line, music, moves and God knows what else, being created on the spot.

I tried to appear professional and act as if I had experience and knew what I was doing. All while trying to remember the sequence of each move to the music. And keeping the boy's hands where they belonged. I hoped that the titles I gave these musical experiments would "tell the story" - Judy Garland and Mickey Rooney live! "I know what we can do! Let's put on a show!"

I have often wondered: What these efforts would have been like if I had *really* studied dance? I knew one girl in school who actually studied ballet, since her mother was able to take her to practice. I admired and craved her posture and poise and the dance positions she would assume when talking to others. In my eyes, she was elegantly beautiful and had all the secrets I was trying to discover on my own.

How sad, or fortunate, that we did not have the easily accessible recording devices that we have now. What I would give to see one of those hopeful events that are still happy and glamorous in my mind.

Maybe it's just as well.

MEMORIES
Diane Torgerson

Have you ever tried to get back to the moment of your own first consciousness . . . the very first thought that you had, that you were aware of? Not just snippets of memory, but the moment that you were aware of being you. How far could you get? Two years old? Two-and-a-half? Three?

In my mind I can vividly recreate my first memory. I am on my hands and knees, no shirt, only short pants. I can feel the soft sun filtering through the palm trees, which are creating a little breeze and making changing shapes on the ground.

I am in the front yard - house to my left, sidewalks and street to the right - and I am dragging my tongue in the sand. It's white and looks as though it will taste like sugar. Eager anticipation quickly turns to disgust and shock. It is dry, gritty and hard to get out of my mouth. How could I have been so wrong?

Our house was a block from the Catholic hospital. Mother would often take me to the end of the driveway and point to the hospital and say that she was going there soon to have a baby and would come home with a baby boy or girl.

This just seemed all "matter of fact" to me. No big deal. I took it upon myself several times to ride my tricycle across the West Palm

Beach Highway and look around this place Mother was going to be. I don't remember her being aware of this. If she had been, I'm certain I'd remember her discipline. Despite being only 4'10" tall, 8-plus months pregnant and paralyzed and spastic on the right side of her body, she made her loving presence known.

Once, while on one of my trike tours, I found a balloon in the street that was tied in a knot. I tried to untie it with my teeth and bit a hole in it. Never did that again.

On hot days, Mother would fill a little bucket with water, which was big enough for me to sit in up to my neck. I would hunker down in there and observe the world from my little cool spot. There were bushes nearby that had hard berries. I was told not to eat them so I stuffed my ears full.

Mother finally brought my sister home. Her crib was in their bedroom, and I was determined to climb in and sit with her. She was tiny, dark-haired. Her little rump was covered with a diaper, sticking up in the air. Always sleeping.

I returned to this house in the 1980s. It was easy to locate because the hospital was still across the street, but the house had become derelict: windows broken, boards falling off, grimy, trash everywhere. But through a window I could see the bedroom where the crib had been; where a relationship that has spanned many decades began.

MIMES
Diane Torgerson

I think that show biz just simply lusts in my heart. I decided, at the age of forty-eight, to put together a mime troupe. I had ordered some study tapes and descriptions of what some known mimes had done and fell in love with it. I was preparing for a new road-show! I found three adventurous women, designed costumes of black-and-white striped shirts, black pants, white gloves, red suspenders and appropriate mime makeup.

I belonged to a church at the time that encouraged the arts in worship and this seemed an appropriate venue to present. Easter was coming in a few months, so I wrote a skit around the agony in the Garden, the betrayal of and the obedience of Christ. I used the Via Delarosa music for the story background. The music was mournful and haunting and seemed perfect. We used red, white and purple scarves to create emotional scenes within scenes.

We practiced and practiced. We watched the mime tapes over and over, using the exercises to learn mime techniques. We practiced our craft in front of senior citizen groups. Unfortunately, in one case, they were all in wheelchairs and various stages of dementia, some being tethered to their chairs. Their caretakers used the momentary entertainment being provided for them to take a coffee break somewhere.

We began our performance and soon became mesmerized by the slow determination of the various men and women who began to remove their clothes - all without making a single sound, like silent zombies. We stopped what we were doing and began going to each person, trying to get them back into their chairs and to stop them from removing their clothing.

They were unbelievably swift in what there were doing! Some were stark naked in what seemed like seconds. I told my friends to keep them from falling because they were beginning to move about the room and I ran to find their helpers.

It was like the facility was deserted. No sound, no person at desks, no one in the halls. We had been abandoned! I finally found them in a small lunch room and explained what was happening. They shot out like cannons and were gone instantly. We left quietly.

Then, unexpectedly, our mismatched training methods and efforts were rescued and a true mime troupe was born. One of the mimes had a friend visiting who was a Broadway actress, traveling as a one-person, one-act, storytelling play of the day of Crucifixion. We begged, pleaded and threw ourselves on her mercy to knit our effort and story together. I'm not too sure she was happy about being cornered because at one point while trying to pull together the mess we were in, I heard her mutter, "I'm and *actress*! I can *do* this!" It was miraculous; she showed us how to develop scenes within scenes, how to move and work together and how to disappear by standing with our backs to the audience.

We really only did one complete performance. Many people were weeping by the end of it. I hope that it was because they saw the story we were trying to tell.

ANDY
Diane Torgersen

It was Christmas Day. I was making a phone call and trying to speak thru a stopped-up nose, while avoiding looking at my red eyes and unhappy face. Our pet of seven years had passed away suddenly. This may sound odd, but the pet was a two-and-a-half pound dwarf bunny we had named Andy . . . a remarkably intelligent, intuitive creature that had totally stolen our hearts.

He was an "impulse buy" at a local pet store. They had set him up with a cage and toys to show the simplicity of owning such a pet. He was tan with tiny charcoal stripes around his body (I later learned that this description identified him as Hungalarian in the rabbit world) and sported sharp, short ears and the requisite white fluffy tail.

The "catch" was that he came over to sniff and lick our fingers. It was meant to be. They told us that it was a female so we named him Annie. Later, we took him to the vet for a check-up. The vet disclosed our error. My husband, while walking thru the waiting room with the cage, proudly announced, "When we came in my rabbit was an Annie. We are going home with an Andy. My rabbit has had a sex change!" Someone said, "Rabbits are like that."

We took him home with a water bottle, food and a few instructions, which we soon discovered were laughably inadequate. He was fearless . . . and bossy from the first. I became his "woman" when he fell in love with a pair of blue fluffy slippers I had. My husband was a tolerated enemy whom he nipped in the face as often as he could. We finally had to have him neutered to reduce the number of scars my husband was collecting.

Andy was incredibly teachable. I bought cat balls that had slits in them and rolled them to him. He would pick up the balls with his teeth and with both front paws, throw them back to me! I had lined up some boxes to contain him one time, and I saw him pacing the perimeter of those boxes, looking right, left and up, back up a few steps and with a mighty leap gracefully sailed over them all. I would not have believed it, if I had not seen it. Those boxes were 18" high and wide.

He was very time oriented. He would put himself to bed at exactly 8:00 PM every night, including making the yearly time changes. What moments of fun he provided, just being himself, tearing around the perimeters of a room with occasional, loud, thudding bangs from those big feet punctuating his progress. When he was entirely pixilated, he would leap high into the air to twist his little body into amazing contortions to show his happiness of the moment.

Did you know that bunnies can purr? And he dearly loved dandelion greens, especially when I hid a little extra surprise food treat in them. He often climbed the stairs to join me in my studio for awhile, during the day. And he always came out to greet any guests.

He had several eye problems for which we took him to an animal oculist. One of those times while we waited for the doctor, I cradled Andy on the examining table. When the oculist walked in, he stood and watched us for a moment and then said, "He knows that he is loved."

Those few words say it all.

CRIME, BURGLARY AND PABLUM
Diane Torgersen

CRIME

Looking back, seven years old can be a very inventive, explorative age. We had just moved to Venice, California during World War II and lived in an upstairs apartment. Mother was pregnant again and less able to keep track of me. There was the ocean to explore, canals to investigate, billboards to climb and streets to ride my new handmade scooter. The area around our apartment lent itself to a life of discovery, exploring, crime and retributions.

About the scooter (my first set of wheels), Dad had made it with a skate taken apart, a board to stand on with the skate parts nailed below, and an upright board with handles for a handsome steering column. Life was never the same once I pushed off.

A school was next door with lots of space to practice wheelies, turns and speed. Most of my friends had one of these handmade traveling boards, so we were busy with races and simply roaming around. Unfortunately, the canals had no guard rails along them and sometimes a kid would ride his scooter into the water. As far as I can remember, there was always someone around to jump in and save them.

This was the same neighborhood where I learned naughty words and practiced them in chalk on the sidewalks. I can still feel the cement under my knees as I crawled around with a rag and a bucket of water, washing all my sins away. This was also the year I taught classes in lighting matches under an abandoned house with two or three of my friends.

I'm not sure who told my mother, but I do remember the really good spanking I got. She tucked me between her legs and whacked me with one of her slippers. Truly, I never did light another match. At least, not in Venice.

BURGLARY

So I found a new hobby: burglary. I really did like ice cream. And we didn't have it as often as I would have liked. So I began to occasionally take a coin or two from the top of my parents' dresser and treat myself to an ice cream bar. I would climb a huge billboard along the street and sit, swinging my legs as I enjoyed the fruits of my labors.

Unfortunately, my sticky fingers expanded their areas of operations. I took some pennies from my parents' friends' home while they were playing cards and put them in the pocket of my dress. When Mother undressed me that night, the pennies fell out. I can still hear the sound of the pennies as they fell to the floor and rolled. I can still consider the silence as both of us looked at the pennies lying around the room. After a moment, Mother asked, "Where did you get those?" with *that look* in her eyes. I never liked to tamper with "The Look." Things only got worse. "I stole them," I admitted.

Mother was always creative with punishment.

In those war years, our sugar came in little white cotton bags with strings attached to pull them shut. My atonement for stealing pennies was to wear those bags on my hands during our evening walks. Every evening my dad came home and after we had had dinner, the family would stroll the beach along a boardwalk. If anyone asked why I was wearing the bags, I was to tell them.

I was grateful for the people who thought I had been burned, these being bandages, and they stopped to offer sympathy. I hoped to let them think that was the reason for both hands being in sacks, but no . . . there is That Look again. "No, ma'am," I'd clarify. "I have to wear these because I stole pennies." Immediately, people straightened up from their bent position of pity to look at my parents, nod, and walk on.

Embarrassment is a great leveler. Along with mortification and humiliation. The golden trinity of raising children.

PABLUM

I wouldn't consider a liking for pablum for the beginning of a life headed for prison, but I couldn't get the idea of eating some out of my head. Mother had finally come home with our baby brother and later was giving him real food. I tasted the cool, creamy substance and craved it from that moment. She stored it in the kitchen, which sat off a back porch that ran the length of the upper story we lived in. This included mine and my sister's shared bedroom. A convenient little alley.

I decided to wait until my parents were asleep and sneak along the porch to the kitchen door, which happened to have a broken pane near the floor. Just my size. I got down and gently stuffed myself into and thru the space; it took awhile. I tried not to make any noise as I found the pablum and scooped a big handful into my mouth.

Hey. Seven-year olds aren't cooks. Who knew it had to be mixed with something liquid? I nearly choked on the dust of it. I couldn't get it out, down or unstuck. There was a bathroom on the way back to my bedroom so my idea was to get there and wash it out. I tried to crawl back thru the same window but got stuck. Stuck in the window with a mouth full of what is now becoming mush. Some angel of mercy awakened my mother. The kitchen light came on and there she stood.

You know, I think we really understood each other that evening. Her part was finally, fully accepting that this unpredictable child was going to be with her for the next eleven years. And my part was being eternally grateful for her early warning systems.

LAUGHTER
Diane Torgersen

What is it in us that makes even a small baby roar with laughter? I watched my six-month old being lifted in the air by a friend who had layers and layers of red, curly hair. When he had his tiny fists buried in her curls, he threw his head back and laughed and laughed and laughed. Where does that come from at such a pre-verbal age?

We all know the laugh that catches us off guard, makes us lose our breath before we can push those explosions of laughter out that leave us helpless and weeping, trying to stop, only to begin again. The feeling bubbles up and it starts all over again. The more spontaneous it is, the harder it is to censor. And it is contagious.

And what is going on during grief? My mother had passed away and relatives were coming to Lake Charles, Louisiana for the service. My dad was driving myself, my sister and our grandmother around the area to fill time. He was describing the reasons for the graves being above ground in the area due to the high water table.

My sister and I were in the back seat. We looked at each other and knew in an instant what was going to happen. We looked away, trying to hold it in. We strangled, trying to stop what was on its way out. No use; it exploded in great peals of sound that were futile to contain. We tried not to look at each other because that only made it worse. Our elegant, southern grandmother gave us looks from the front seat that under normal circumstances would have have left scorch marks where our bodies had been. But that only made it worse.

I have tried to discover what was going on at that moment. I can say only that it was healing. There obviously is something healing in laughter. Even inappropriate laughter.

But why? And how? It's an activity that almost defies definition or explanation. It's powerful. We can read that it produces endorphins that make us feel good. It can reduce pain and help us past rough spots. It's memorable. We're willing to pay money for comedians to tickle us with their verbal descriptions. How about legendary "roasts" of celebrities that are deliberate titillations that can cause roars of laughter?

What about someone else's pain? I recently saw an episode on television that featured a chef traveling around the world, being required to eat whatever was offered to him. He admitted to having eaten something disagreeable during that episode and also had a segment set up in which he was to submit to an Asian massage and spa treatments. These included small Mason jars being suctioned onto his back and being walked on by tiny Asian women who were also able to contort his body into positions not normally doable. The silent, pleading look on his face was what did me in. I laughed until it was no longer possible to stand up and or talk.

We human beings are indeed fearfully and wonderfully and strangely made.

SENG
Diane Torgersen

We gave our dog away. How could we have done that? What kind of people were we?!

I'll tell you what we were. We were five intimidated, clueless, un-dog-trained, miserable, seemingly hapless humans.

It seemed like an answer to an empty spot in our family to get a puppy for our three-year-old son. The two older boys were in school and he only had the companionship of Jemima, a neighbor child who lived on the other side of the hedges. So one day we excitedly drove through the English countryside to look at pups. Four beautiful Lhasa Apsos - little, tan fur balls - were bouncing around inside a pen.

We were overwhelmed by the history being told to us by the owner-breeders. These were not ordinary pups. They were descended from royalty. Literally. Their lineage had been inside China for thousands of years (we were told) and only in recent times were some being allowed outside the country. They were raised to be companions, to roam palaces and sit inside the long sleeves of clothing to keep the owners warm.

Lion Dogs. Dignified, royal, respected. Those words would come back to haunt us.

The first mistake was in not studying how to raise, train and live with a dog. We thought past experiences would be enough. Enthusiasm carried us along for awhile until the reality of living and getting on with our lives took over. What a beautiful thing he was - perfectly majestic with a lovely, furry body. He was also lively, fun and almost barkless.

But Seng had a dark side. And we had stupid sides. His outranked ours. We absolutely could not housebreak him. He piddled on everything in sight: walls, floors, beds, clothing - even people's legs - were targets. We walked that little dog so much that he was trembling to strain one more little squirt out to dominate the world with his scent. And then would come home to wet in inappropriate spots once more. We yelled "On the paper!" at him so often that it became a cliché. We would almost have fistfights before entering the house because it was an unwritten rule that whoever saw the mess first had to clean it up.

We had high hopes for a couple who often babysat the boys when we made trips. In their younger years they had raised, trained and housebroken pups before sending them home with the new owners. They worked the entire week with Seng, and pronounced him a "Dirty Dog" when we returned. Apparently, that's where the term "Dirty Dog" came from - a pet who is impossible to housebreak.

We begged people for help and information; Brits are known for their well-trained and obedient dogs. The last straw was when Seng climbed up onto one of the beds and did a big pile of business there.

Coward that I was, I put an ad in the local newspaper: "Child allergic to dog. Free to a good home." Never mind that Lhasa Apsos are hypoallergenic since they have hair, not fur. For some reason, he had no further problems from that moment. We wondered if he had read the ad in the papers on the kitchen floor: "Let's see...Dog food is a good price this week - I can continue to eat. There is a Fair downtown on the weekend. Wait! What's this? A dog-giveaway?!!!"

A kind, portly German lady responded to the ad and came to see him. She was a "walker," she said, who loved to walk the hills and needed a companion. *Perfect!* I thought. He would have endless opportunities to do what he needed. She took him and I called occasionally to see how they were doing. "Wonderful," she said in a strong German accent, "We have many walks. And I take him to the butchers where I buy him ox cheeks!"

That little dog must have thought he had moved into heaven. He finally had the circumstances to show that he *could* be dignified, royal and respectable.

Ox cheeks. Who would have thought of that?

HALLOWEEN BUNNIES
Diane Torgersen

While living in England for three years, I had more available time to do as I pleased. It was different to fill my days with unusual activities and to be able to choose what I was going to do each day. Perhaps I had a little too much free time.

I had three sons who at that time were four, twelve and fourteen. The American holiday of Halloween was coming up and they needed costumes for individual parties, as did I. After having gone as a ghost the year before, I decided to try a different approach. The ghost had been easy, with two eye holes cut appropriately in a white sheet and a sheer layer of material over it that wafted around when moving.

But this particular year I thought I would make a fluffy pink bunny outfit. It was on the order of a Playboy Bunny, with a big fluffy tail and a head piece with huge pink ears. I found the longest, most sappy-looking eyelashes to wear. That plus high heels, lacy hose and I was good to go.

The twelve-year old decided that he would like to wear the costume also. He was about my size so with dark leggings, his grimy tennis shoes and dark ghoulish make-up, he was a perfect teenage-zombie pink bunny. My four-year old also wanted to wear the bunny outfit. I padded it out so he was a plump little bunny, with whiskers and a cherub face. Adorable. I have to brag a little - all three outfits won

First Prize at all their parties.

The first Halloween, I took only the oldest boy out trick-or-treating as his brother had a cold and could not go. I worked then and had gotten home late and buying costumes was not an option in the 1960s. I told my anxious son that we had to find something around the house for him to wear. So help me, the fastest thing I could come up with was a Carmen Miranda look. A bowl of plastic fruit on our table gave me the idea.

Bandana on the head, fruit pinned to that, a large shirt over his coat (it was cold outside) and a long skirt, flashy make-up and we stepped outside. The biggest blessing he had going for him was that no one recognized him. The lure of all that chocolate and candy being given away made him desperate enough to wear anything. Thank goodness his father wasn't home yet to ask if I had lost my mind.

Another year I made huge spiders out of wrapping paper tubes and almost asphyxiated myself while painting them black in the garage. I hung three of them on the small entry porch and the two oldest boys sat on the top of the porch and manipulated them as small children dressed as creatures came to the door.

It was too realistic - most of them screamed and ran, including one little Superman who retreated with his cape flying behind him. I chased after them all and filled their bags generously with Halloween sweets and apologies.

MILE MARKER 462
Diane Torgersen

It was 1962. We were making a military move from San Antonio, Texas to Anchorage, Alaska with our eighteen-month-old son and had decided to drive the Alaskan Highway (the ALCAN) for the scenic experience. We made one stop in Wyoming to visit with my parents and then entered Canada to make our way to Mile Marker 1 to begin our journey thru the wilderness.

The road was comprised of gravel that year. And big hunks of them. There were huge road graders working all the time to keep them evenly spread. The views were magnificent around every bend in the road: mountains, tall pines, northern trees, gracious panoramas off in the distance around huge boulders and rocks. Rivers, streams, deer and bears could be seen. Not too many people were traveling then; it was exciting to pass someone going south. The time of year was May so the weather was beautiful, if getting colder.

I can't tell you how long it would have taken us to drive the entire highway to Anchorage because as I was driving in the 400 Mile Markers, I hit a rock in the road. I had been driving on the left side of the road because a grader was working on the right. When a car came toward us, I attempted to cross over the heap of gravel down the middle of the road to get back into my lane. There just happened to be a huge boulder right there under the gravel, which my car got hung up on. The worker on the grader came to try to help us, but nothing worked. We flagged down someone going north to ask that they alert an inn up ahead about five miles, that we needed assistance.

Someone did come, in a short time. This apparently happened a lot. They arranged for our car to be towed to Lake Muncho Lodge at Mile Marker 462 for evaluation. Once there, a mechanic eventually came from one of the far-spaced gas stations along the highway to see if he could help. The diagnosis: all motor mounts were broken and the driveshaft was history. It could have been worse. Except we were in the middle of proverbial nowhere with very few car parts departments. One of the workers at the lodge even asked that the mechanic take the driveshaft off his own car to see if it would fit ours. A gracious gesture, but it didn't work. The motor mounts didn't seem to be an issue. Nothing to do but contact Detroit and order another driveshaft. It would arrive by bus. The bus only came by once a day.

My husband notified Elmendorf Air Force Base of our predicament and we stayed to wait for the bus each day.

Now, despite our worry about repairing the car, this was a beautiful area for this to have happened. Muncho Lake was across the road, with mountains and trees all around. Although we were warned about the bears and other dangerous creatures that roamed out back. The lodge had a bar and restaurant, rustic rooms and surprisingly, a very loyal clientele of daily visitors who lived back in the woods and came out for nourishment and drinks with friends. Some of them adopted us and took us to the few entertainment spots in the area. One was a hot springs pool of water hidden way back in the hills.

One afternoon we couldn't locate our eighteen-month old. We looked in the usual places since he had made himself at home in the lodge and everyone knew him. After a very short time of not finding him, we all began to panic. The back door of the kitchen was left standing open and he could have wandered out. A bear had been spotted in the area the night before. And then there was the lake across the street. People were running in all directions trying to find him. We called and called his name to no avail. I was standing in the kitchen trying to catch my breath and think what to do next when I heard a delicate little "clink." He was sitting on the floor behind a big door. There was a crate of empty beer bottles back there and he was systematically drinking the leftovers and gently putting the bottles back. He took a really good nap that day.

After waiting and meeting the daily bus for a week, we ultimately had to finish our trip to Anchorage on the bus. What an experience that was. The driver was part tour guide and often stopped by the road so we could see or watch something going on, such as a herd of elk eating in a field; bears ambling along the road or just a special, beautiful scene before us. Once he stopped alongside of the Dahl Mountains to see if we could catch a glimpse of the elusive Dahl sheep. Which we did. How nice to have someone else doing the driving.

My husband returned about a week later after the car part arrived, to drive the car on to Anchorage. For a 1955 Buick sedan, it performed in an excellent manner thru the next three years of brutal Alaskan winters before being driven across Canada and back to San Antonio, Texas via Tennessee when we changed bases again.

NEW YEAR'S EVE
Diane Torgersen

You know, after the clock strikes 12:00 AM, it's pretty much over. At one New Year's Eve party, I glanced at my husband after midnight and was startled by the fact that he was holding one eye open with his fingers while apparently trying to sleep with the other one.

We were in the basement of someone's home in Anchorage, Alaska. The room was very typical for a couple in our age group; it was made up to be a "den" - very comfy with overstuffed furniture, a small fireplace and a bar/kitchen. The 1960s music was loud, conversations even more so. The fireplace, while picturesque, was beginning to heat up the room.

All of us had traveled thru -32 degree temperatures to get here and were suitably dressed should any outdoor emergency arrive. Trays of food were passed around. Unfortunately, everyone smoked back then, so the room was filling with acrid cigarette smoke, guests were getting mellow due to Happy New Year's drinks, sweat was beginning to be a problem so most were shedding heavy hand-knitted sweaters and maybe even a few boots.

Just about the time we had all hit a new level of heat and alcohol endurance, there was a new odor in the room. I wasn't sure what it was, but the room was suddenly wet-dog steamy, and not from the woolen sweaters.

The hosts had put a big pot of black-eyed peas on the stove to cook. Think about it: that's not an odor that goes well with food, steam, alcohol and an already overstimulated tummy. All you long for is a breath of fresh air. Even air that is -32 degrees and will freeze the inside of your nose (which might have been an advantage).

But there was no escaping. The hosts maintained that it was traditional to eat those peas on New Year's Eve to ensure prosperity in the coming year. Unfortunately, they took an inordinate amount of time to finish cooking. How terrific it would have been if they had been cooked beforehand. Or even if they had put some ham or sausage in for seasoning. Anything but that stark aroma. Sniffing ham or sausage would have been preferable to the peas.

Sitting around, wishing to go home to your bed, long after midnight, when the evening is truly past its function and intention, is not a good thing. Especially with every nook and cranny filled with the aroma of fresh black-eyed peas still cooking. I was ready to give up any prosperity for the year just to be able to go home.

Another New Year's was spent on board a luxury cruise ship. Beautifully decorated for the holiday seasons, it was loaded with every festivity by both the cruise company and the people who were on board. Every costume and tradition of the season were welcome on board and fleshed out by the ship's crews and cooks: magnificent meals, entertainment and activities. Everyone was working hard to impress and entertain.

The biggest event of the cruise, of course, was New Year's Eve. Everyone dressed for the evening and the dining rooms were resplendent with extravagantly prepared meals and dishes. The guests were twinkling with sparkles in their hair and clothing; there was soft pink lighting that made everyone look thirty years younger and we all fell under the spell.

We gorged and indulged and then did it again. We were stuffed full of what I can only wish to remember but can only come up with the impression that was made: lovely, ornate, aromatic, creative, glorious foods. As for we, the participants: think of geese being prepared to make paté. At least, that's what I felt like at the end of the evening.

In all fairness, we did know about the midnight Chocolate Extravaganza that the cooks had probably spent months preparing. There were tables and tables of every chocolate fantasy you could possibly imagine: waterfalls, candies, cakes, statues - every chocolate-coated thing known to man. Faces, fairies, storybook characters and amazing artwork drizzled and fizzled and twirled everywhere.

It all reminded me of my little dauschund who, if she could find enough food, would eat until she looked as though she would explode. When she would escape and rummage thru garbage cans, her skin would become so tight that I thought if I touched her she would rip like a zipper.

That's how I felt at that moment at the chocolate buffet. *Don't touch*!

Gluttony is never a pretty sight.

And I felt that I was too old to be making such obviously bad food decisions. But New Year's always gives one the hope of redemption.

OAK RIDGE, TENNESSEE: THE SECRET CITY
Diane Torgersen

The houses are what I remember first - they were lined up and down all the streets, exactly alike: square, gray, little flat-topped boxes, one beside the other. Hundreds of them, with long boardwalks built across and on top of the red clay to access the street and cars parked on the gravel road and to also reach the coal bins at the end of the boardwalks. There was character to them, simply in the number of them and their sameness. Standing alone, one would have looked forgotten, odd snd unfinished, but together they looked significant.

The year was 1942. Oak Ridge (unnamed at the time) was to be a secret city that would participate in the building of the atomic bomb that would ultimately end World War II.

Consider the planning, construction and operation of a military reservation. As an example, say that someone would contact a Holiday Inn company and ask them to: Buy up sixty acres in the foothills of eastern Tennessee. In six months' time, have land cleared and utilities installed. Build homes in eight months for the 20,000 families who would arrive there. Provide restaurants, schools, water, electricity, transportation, medical facilities and a local newspaper. The population would increase to 75,000 in one-and-a-half years and would be fed, housed, educated and transported to and from work. And most importantly, *no one is to know about it*!

That is exactly what happened at Black Oak Ridge: It already had rail lines, was a safe distance from the coast, had high ridges (to muffle possible explosions and hide the working plants from saboteurs) and dams for electricity. Perfect.

The square-box houses were prefabricated and came in three sections. They had a living/dining room area dominated by a pot-bellied coal stove, a kitchen, a bathroom and on the other side, two bedrooms separated by a small closet in which my mother kept the washing machine that had to be rolled into the kitchen to use. The very basic of needs for a family of five. The flooring was comprised of sheets of masonite screwed down and showed stains, much to my mother's dismay. Rugs were an immediate necessity for warmth and appearance.

The population would ultimately grow to 75,000 with 10,000 dwelling units near a work area one-and-a-half miles wide and six-and-a-half miles long. Workers were recruited from all over the nation and *not* told what they were going to be doing. Staff was brought in to design the community centers, banks, post office, bus terminals, clothing stores, ten-cent stores, movie theaters, supermarkets, bowling alleys and football fields.

Children grew up "behind a fence" in the shadow of the world's most secretive undertaking. It was a diverse population with varied socioeconomic levels. The community was youthful (the adult ages ranged from thirty to forty years old) and held the highest birth rate in the nation. There were no class distinctions and education was progressive or modern. There was an openness to religion - Methodists and Baptists shared the same building. Among the Jews, Catholics and Protestants, there was cooperation and understanding.

No one was allowed to own property, but only rent for $30-$85 a month. Because it was a military reservation, parents had little reason to fear for the safety of children. They were never afraid, had great freedom and roamed the hills. Children ten years or older had passes to get in or out of the reservation, which had gates that were armed by patrols.

Behind our house were woods covering a hill which was a great discovery since we had never seen anything like them in Venice, California. And roam we did. We found a stream at the bottom of the hill, saw foxes and played hide-and-seek in the trees. We caught June bugs, tied a length of thread around their little bodies and instantly had our own tiny flying kites.

On one side of us was a family who seemed to live differently than mine did. I think their father was one of the engineers. The boy and girl were always neat and their clothes pressed. Her hair was always curled and in ribbons. He wore a little belt with his shorts. They never went barefoot - something that we were quickly becoming fond of. They introduced themselves by all three of their names - first, middle and last. Looking back, I can only think their mother must have thought we were urchins. I peeked thru their screened door once to see their table set for lunch: placemats, silverware, napkins and glasses of iced tea with a lemon slice. I was mesmerized.

We usually had a dish, a paper napkin and a sandwich that we picked up from the kitchen. Ours was a communal effort; their children seemed to be waited on by their parents. A new look at another life.

The size and type of the homes were given by family size. There were four movie theaters, six recreation halls, bowling alleys, twenty-three tennis courts, a swimming pool, ball parks, taverns and a 9,400-volume library. There was a little drama theater, music society, concerts and community sings. All free. For a fee, one could use the skating rink, amusement parks and art school.

Most of these amenities and social understandings were absent from the little town we moved to after the war was over, just fifteen miles away. Gone was the pool, little theater, concerts, art school, amusement park and movie theater. Present were divisions and segregation of people and religions.

EARTHQUAKE
Diane Torgersen

It was dusky outside; that time of day when the sun is still lighting objects but shadows are beginning to deepen and lengthen. It's about 5:30 PM in Anchorage, Alaska on Good Friday Eve. I was standing outside the back entrance to the private x-ray department at which I worked, waiting for my husband and two children to pick me up.

We had lived in Anchorage almost three years and we had often experienced rumblings of the earth. But this was different. This started with a low moan and a gentle waving of the ground. The moan became louder and the waves more pronounced, as if they were moving across an ocean. The doctor I worked for ran outside just as the ground was beginning to pitch wildly, making the cars nearby rock up and down and back and forth as if they were floating on water. We kept falling down and helping each other back up. The noise was so loud that we couldn't hear each other speak. Pieces of materials were beginning to fall off the building.

Other sounds were the telephone wires zinging as the poles pitched back and forth, like ship spars in a wild ocean and explosions as transformers blew up. In the distance, we could see dark clouds of dust as houses imploded and fell.

I wondered where my husband was and what was happening to him and our two- and four-year olds.

He had just entered my one-story medical building and was in a hallway, carrying one child and holding the other by his hand. As the earthquake intensified, the walls touched them on both sides. He turned and tried to run outside. A wall leaned on him at one point, but he exited finally with both children screaming. One had lost a boot and was hysterical about it.

The quake lasted 4.5 minutes and was a 9.2 on the Richter Scale - the second-most powerful one to ever happen. We learned later that lakes in Texas sloshed around in their beds, and that the entire earth rang like a bell.

We were able to drive the few miles to our home, avoiding holes and cracks in the roads. The electricity was out but our home was standing. Eventually, the radio said that the water in our area was safe. The inside of the house looked like it had been violently shaken - everything was out of the closets and drawers, the furniture was askew and the washer and dryer were across the room. Every piece of china, glass and crystal was broken.

People behave differently when there is a disaster. We invited two other families to stay with us for three days, one of them had indeed lost their home. For some reason, we all wanted to be in the same room together. We slept in chairs, sofas, sleeping bags and blankets, making beds for the five children in corners of the rooms.

The aftershocks were nerve-racking. We learned later that many homes along the Cook Inlet were swallowed up or fell into the bay. One of the worst events was the tsunami that struck Seward, Alaska about twenty-five miles east of us. Seward was built around a small bay and when the tsunami entered the area, it swirled in a flushing motion, carrying everything on the rim to the bottom of the water. This included trains and tracks, homes and businesses.

Since Sunday was Easter, the other mothers and I hid Easter Eggs, baskets and goodies all around the house for the children to find that morning. Even in the midst of disaster, we wanted to do something that felt normal.

When writing the story of your life, don't let anyone else hold the pen.
Anonymous

Charlotte Hackman is an author, playwright, and actress who has lived in Wilmington, North Carolina since 1993. She grew up in Jefferson City, Missouri, got her undergraduate degree in English and speech from Central Missouri State University and a Masters in Psychology from Texas A&M University.

Charlotte taught English, speech and drama in Texas schools before working as a family counselor. She has been very active in the Landfall community and was instrumental organizing the Landfall Writers' Group. Much of Charlotte's writing is done during the summer months spent on Sugar Mountain in western North Carolina.

She and her husband Ed, enjoy golf and tennis, reading and travel, and spending time with family. Charlotte and Ed have one son, Colin, seen from time to time on WECT as the weather man. He and his wife Michelle have a six-year-old daughter, Peyton.

The Strength to Let Go is Charlotte's first non-fiction book, published in 2015 under the pen name Jo Henry. Her play, *Change of Life* was produced off-Broadway in New York as well as in Wilmington. Major movies, TV series and numerous stage credits are included in her acting resume. She is currently working on a mystery novel and a collection of short plays.

BATHROOM MISUNDERSTANDING
Charlotte Hackman

I don't normally take long driving trips by myself, but I was going to meet a friend for a three-day reunion in the North Carolina mountains. I armed myself with snacks and a small cooler filled with soft drinks and some CDs with my favorite 1960s music. I was snacking and drinking and singing my way down the highway when the urge hit me. I needed a bathroom and I needed it sooner rather than later.

The sign read, "Rest Stop 2 Miles." I looked at my speedometer and nudged my speed a bit to get there faster. I pulled into the parking lot, got out, locked the car, and headed for the lady's room. It had a sign that read "Out of Order." *How could they advertise a rest stop where the ladies room is out of order?*

I don't know if men have this issue, but when my mind says I can go potty soon, my body totally expects to get it done...soon. The minute I pull into my driveway at home, it is a given, the first stop in the house will be the bathroom. *And now the ladies room was not available!*

I looked around and realized no one else was there, so I went around to the Men's Room. I knocked just to be sure, but I heard nothing, so I went in. There was the urinal, but of course I headed for the stall with the door. With great relief I began the ritual of taking down my pants, trying desperately to keep my pant legs from hitting the floor while I balanced above the commode. At least men can stand straight up at a urinal. I always hear Mom's voice from my childhood warning me *not* to sit on a public toilet seat. *Has anyone ever actually gotten a venereal disease from a toilet seat?*

As I juggled my purse and my pants and reached for the toilet paper roll, I heard the bathroom door open. Now I wasn't alone. I saw a man's shoes and hoped he didn't look at mine.

"Beautiful day out there," he said. "I been on the road for a long time. Needed to drain my radiator. How about you?"

Was I going to have to answer him? Maybe he'll leave soon. Finally, I pitched my voice a little lower and said, "Yup."

"I been in that pick-up five hours and have five more to go. You know of any good places to eat close to the highway?"

Oh great, a talker. "Nope," I said again with my lowered voice.

I peeked out of the stall. Maybe I could just slide around his back and dash out the door. I was feeling totally embarrassed at this point. I made my move just as he turned around with his hand on his zipper. I froze. *Why didn't I just keep going?* But I just stood there as he looked me up and down.

Oh my God, I'm stuck in the men's room with a sexual predator! Frightening pictures of what might happen next flashed through my head like a horror movie. But I still couldn't move.

"Hot dang, I forgot I'm in North Carolina," he said as he continued checking me out from head to toe. "You're the first one of…you know…uh, your kind I've seen."

"What?" I managed to stammer. What did being in North Carolina have to do with anything? Didn't they have women where he came from?

"And you look really good. I mean uh… for a…uh…" Now he was at a loss for words.

He really didn't appear to be very threatening. I no longer felt in danger, but I was still standing frozen against the wall when I said, "I'm so sorry. I just really had to go and I forgot to lock the door."

"Oh no, it's perfectly okay. I'm a law-abiding man, and see you are, too. I understand you didn't have a choice but to come in here. No harm. 'Specially since we were both born with the same equipment." He was now the one who seemed embarrassed and trying to make light of an awkward situation, but I was a little confused.

"No, I just *had* to come in here and use this bathroom because I couldn't use the other one." And then it occurred to me what he was thinking. "Oh God," I gasped.

"No it's okay, really. I totally understand it's the law." He reached out and gave my shoulder a little punch like guys do. "Oh sorry. Maybe ya'll don't do that." He folded his arms across his body not knowing what to do next. Well, I didn't know what to do either. I honestly didn't know whether to laugh or cry. I was just glad he wasn't the bad guy I had guessed him to be earlier.

"I hope you don't mind me asking, but I'm just naturally the curious type. Have you had any surgeries yet, cause you look like a real woman…uh, and well… those look dang good, too." He was staring straight at my chest.

"No! I mean *yes*, these are mine. I *am* a real woman," I tried to explain.

"Of course you're a woman…if you want to be. I didn't mean to offend you. You just have to understand I'm not familiar with your kind. I'm tryin' to keep an open mind. Live and let live…that's what I say."

"Well, yes, I agree, but I'm not that kind…not one of… *not* whatever you might be thinking..."

He interrupted me. "I get it. The law says you had to use this bathroom because of your birth certificate. For what it's worth, I honestly don't think you would be a threat in the Ladies' Room. Who would even know if you were in a stall?"

"Of course I'm not a threat! I had to use *this* bathroom because I couldn't go in the other one and I was desperate." This whole conversation was getting crazy. "Now, I really need to go!"

"Again? Lordy you might have an enlarged prostate. It'll cause you to feel like you have to pee again right after you just did. My daddy had that issue. Go right ahead and try." He gestured toward the urinal.

"I don't have a prostate!" I shouted at him.

"Well fine, that's why I asked you if you already had the surgery. Now I guess they gave you a tiny bladder just like a woman." He was laughing now.

"Seriously, I have to go…leave. And I'm not…I don't have a…oh, never mind," I said.

"Yes sir…uh, ma'am. See, I'm catching on to this thing. Wait 'til I tell the folks at home I shared a bathroom with one of your kind in North Carolina. They will never believe it. Guess this was just my lucky day after all. Can I take a picture with you?" he asked seriously.

"*No!*" I responded harshly as I rushed past him.

"Have a nice day, and tell your surgeon he did a fantastic job. Shucks, I'd a never guessed if you hadn't been in the men's room," he said as I left. And then I heard him say to himself, "Dang, he looked just like a woman to me."

I swear, I will never go into another Men's Room as long as I live… at least not in North Carolina.

BATHROOM COUNSELING
Charlotte Hackman

We pulled into the gas station to fill up and of course I had to go to the ladies' room. We were on our way to Missouri to visit family and it was a dreaded two-day trip that my husband and I do every year. Not that we dreaded seeing family, but neither of us enjoy long days in the car.

I went in while he was going through the ritual of getting the gas. Shortly after entering my stall, I heard someone else enter and I could see her spike heels under the door. As she went into the adjoining stall, she dropped her purse and was cursing and mumbling to herself. Her lipstick rolled under into my space and I grabbed it and handed it back under the wall. She didn't say anything for a while and then she asked if I could hear her.

"Uh, yes I can hear you," I replied.

"Thank God. I really need to talk." She sounded young and desperate, so I said OK.

"I'm having the day from hell! The honest-to-God day from *hell*!" She sounded really frustrated.

"Oh, I'm so sorry," I replied. I thought perhaps this young lady might need a little consoling, and with my experience as a trained counselor, who better to lend a listening ear. And besides, I was sort of a captive audience for the moment anyway.

She continued, "I thought I was going to pee in my pants before I got in here. My head is killing me and I just want to scream."

"Try taking a few deep breaths and just relax. That always…"

She interrupted me in mid-sentence. "Really! Let me tell you what happened."

I was right, this girl needed a little motherly love. "Okay, if you think that will help," I offered.

"I thought I would surprise Jeff this morning with an early morning visit."

Now I had to wonder, who's Jeff?

She continued, "It was a surprise all right! I have a key and unlocked the door thinking I would just slip into his bed. Well, get this!" she said. "There wasn't room, because some hussy was already in his bed!"

I'm thinking to myself, I bet that was a big surprise for everyone involved. This was beginning to be a story that might need a different kind of consoling than you get from talking to a motherly listening ear.

"I screamed, Jeff screamed and that bitch just covered up her head. Big damn surprise…for me! Can you believe it?"

"Oh my," was all I could manage to say at that point. And with that, I flushed my commode and decided this counseling session might need to come to an end for me.

She continued to rant as I headed to the sink to wash my hands. "I said, 'What the hell is going on here?' And he just kept saying, 'Calm down honey, I can explain.' 'What's to explain?' I yelled. 'You have another woman in your bed!' I totally lost it." She was a little out of breath at that point.

So I said, "That had to be disconcerting, I'm sure."

"I wanted to kill the bitch! Pull her hair out. Punch her in the face."

I guess my comment had been a bit of an understatement. So I tried another approach. "I understand, you were really angry and understandably so. I hope your day gets better but I should probably…"

She interrupted again. "No, listen to this! I was so totally pissed, I threw the lamp at his head and marched right out of there. I slammed the door so hard it might have broken."

I wasn't sure if she was referring to breaking the door, his head or the lamp. "I hope no one was hurt," I said as I reached for a paper towel to dry my hands. I thought it was time for me to leave.

"I was so hurt. What should I do now?" she asked in a rather pitiful voice.

Now I was caught up again. How could I just walk out when she was asking me for help? "Well, maybe just give yourself a little time to cool off. This is obviously very fresh pain." There was silence from the next stall, so I went on, "And then perhaps you can talk to Jeff and work things out." I thought that was sound advice and a good stopping point and I reached for the door handle.

"I don't ever want to see him again." Now she started to cry.

"Oh, don't cry. He's just not worth your tears, honey, if he's going to be unfaithful. Better to find out what a loser he is now before it's too late." *So much for my objective listening ear.*

"But I think I love him," she sobbed.

"Now that's a problem. Maybe it was better when you were angry at him," I said as much to myself as to her. I knew I should probably leave... and I wanted to leave, but my nurturing instincts were working overtime.

She started again through her tears. "I never saw her face. She jerked the sheet over her head. I hope the lamp hit *her*."

"Well, he's the one who let her into his bed, so bash him," I offered, losing all professional counseling demeanor. I was getting way too caught up in this tale of woe.

"Don't call him a bastard! It was that bitch in his bed that's causing the problem!" she yelled.

Now I was at a loss for words. There was a brief silence and then she said the strangest thing.

"Wait a minute, do you know who was in his bed?"

"Who me? Lord, no. I don't know Jeff, or you... so how could I know who was in his bed?" This was getting weird.

"You know, don't you? Tell me! I want to know! I need to know." She was sounding hysterical and suddenly I was the target of her anger.

"Calm down, honey. You're not making sense. Breathe, just breathe." I was trying to remain calm and soothing.

She actually seemed to get a little control when she said, "Listen, you need to tell me who was in Jeff's bed. You're my friend, my *best* friend."

"I've never even met you! I just had to go to the bathroom and you came in here all hysterical. I've been trying to help but I think I should go now. Do you want me to call someone for you?"

"Please don't leave me hanging. If you know, just tell me. Can't you feel my pain? I need you to be my friend." Now she was sounding desperate again.

"I'm sorry, but I don't think I can help. I have to go. My husband is waiting out in the car by now. Do you want me to get the lady who works here? She might know who to call," I asked rather feebly. "Who?" She was yelling now as she flushed her commode. "*No*! I'll kill her. I will kill her!"

Had this girl gone completely mad? What in the world had I gotten into? I finally managed to say in a shaky voice, "I think you need professional help. And I'm not it!"

"Hold on a sec," she said. "Hey, could you keep it down over there?"

"What?" I was totally confused. "Me? You want me to be quiet now?"

"Yes, you. I can't even think straight with your babbling."

"My babbling? You…you said you needed to talk. I was just trying to help. You seemed so …needy." This was too bazaar for words.

"What the hell are you talking about? Look lady, I've had a really bad day and it's not even noon yet. I don't need any more crap on my plate. So just shut up and leave me alone." She actually banged her fist on the wall of her stall!

It was most definitely time for me to leave. We nearly collided as she came out of the stall holding a cell phone to her ear.

"I'm sorry, Michelle, this old lady in the next stall has been talking to herself ever since I came in here and called you. Seriously… just blabbing the whole damn time I've been talking to you. God, you find all kinds of weirdos in a public bathroom."

She looked at me, checked her lipstick in the mirror smeared on some lip gloss and never missed a beat. "So it was Melanie in his bed! I should have known! What a loser! I'm definitely gonna kick *her* butt and I'm totally done with him. I'm over it! Hey, you wannna hang out tonight?" And with that she opened the door and left the ladies room.

She had been on her cell phone with her friend Michelle the entire time I thought she was talking to me. And I was the weirdo in the ladies' room! Perhaps I needed counseling.

THE WHITE ROSES
Charlotte Hackman

My dad was well known in our Missouri neighborhood and beyond as "the rose man" because of his extraordinary rose garden. Every spring the triangular right front corner of our yard would burst into brilliant, beautiful blooms from his beloved rose bushes.

On Memorial Day we would cover Ball jars with foil, and Dad would prepare bouquets to place on deceased family members' graves. That tradition of placing fresh flowers has given way, over the years, to plastic or silk flowers and wreaths. In many cases, my generation has stopped being "grave tenders" all together.

When my brother and his wife moved back to our home town and bought their first house, Dad planted some climbing roses along the right side as a housewarming gift. Unfortunately, neither my brother nor I seemed to inherit Dad's green thumb or his love of gardening, so Dad diligently pruned and fertilized the roses but much to his disappointment, they didn't bloom.

The bushes looked healthy and had green leaves and strong stems, but no blooms. Dad finally thought perhaps the soil just wasn't fit for the roses even though he had added topsoil, fertilizer and plant food every year. He doesn't give up easily and that climbing rose was proving to be his horticultural challenge. After a few years of his best efforts, he finally left it to bloom on its own if it was going to… but it didn't. Everyone sort of forgot about the climbing rose.

Dad had always been a healthy and robust guy, though admittedly more than a little overweight. Tending his vegetable and flower gardens was his major source of exercise and his time-consuming hobby in his retirement. In May, I got the scary phone call from my brother that Dad had suffered a heart attack. I flew home to Missouri with fear in my heart that he might not survive.

I was able to visit with him for four days in intensive care, and even then he was everyone's favorite patient with his jovial demeanor. I believed he was going to recover, but on the evening of the fourth day, we lost him. It was heartbreaking and we were filled with sadness.

We finally left the hospital to go home to my brother's house to try to sleep. When we pulled into the driveway, the headlights caught the side of their house. My sister-in-law, Jackie, said, "What's all that white stuff on the side of the house?" It looked like a bunch of tissues had blown across the yard and stuck there.

"It's late and we're tired. I'll clean it up in the morning," my brother said, as we got out of the car.

Jackie was curious as she walked around to the side to take a closer look. Just as my brother and I were about to go inside, she called out to us.

"Oh, my God, you have to come here. *Now!*" Her voice sounded strained and filled with emotion.

What in the world could have happened? Had she fallen down? We rushed around the house and in the moonlight we could see what had caused her tearful reaction.

There against the side of the house was the climbing rose bush full of beautiful white blooms shining in the moonlight. The three of us just stood there in awe. And then the tears fell and we hugged one another, knowing in our hearts this was a fitting farewell from Dad.

That night, standing there in the moonlight with the white roses, lifted my spirits and filled my heart with joy…and it made me smile on one of the saddest days of my life. Was it truly a message from Dad? That's what I believe.

And the rose never bloomed again.

GETTING "UNSQUARED"
Charlotte Hackman

I grew up in the Sixties in the heartland of the Midwest. Occasionally, I'm asked what drugs I did in my youth. I'm hesitant to answer, but not for the reasons you might think. My answer is just not very *cool,* a term used frequently in the sixties. My drugs were Midol and aspirin. I know, not very *hip*.

In 1969, my husband, Ed and I moved to New York where he commuted into New York City for his job at the home office of a large chemical company and I taught high school English in Suffern, New York. We were very young and very naïve.

One day the conversation in the teachers' lounge turned to the topic of smoking pot. One of my fellow teachers had smelled pot smoke in the girls' bathroom. As the conversation progressed among the mostly young teachers, I made the comment, "I wouldn't have a clue what pot smelled like," and the room went silent. Everyone turned to look at me.

"What?" I asked. *Were they waiting for me to say something else?* "I've never been around anyone who was smoking pot or doing any kind of drugs…at least not that I knew about."

"Seriously?" asked Bill, a math teacher who was engaged to an English teacher in our school.

"Yes, honestly," I answered.

The lounge broke into lots of chatter about how anyone my age could be that sheltered. I even overheard one comment, "How could she be that *square?*" That was not a flattering term in the Sixties, and was replaced later by the term "nerd."

Had everyone in that room smoked pot except me? Was I really *square*? These were my colleagues - the educated educators - readily admitting they could easily recognize the smell of pot smoke! I'd always been a rule follower and proud of it until that moment. Now I just felt…uninformed.

"Don't you think you should at least know how to recognize drugs when you see or smell them?" asked Bill. "It's almost part of our job."

"Really?" I replied. Maybe we should have gone to Woodstock a few weeks prior and I wouldn't have found myself feeling so under experienced. Did I really need to know how pot smelled or made you feel to be a good teacher?

Later in the day, Bill's fiancé, Betty, approached me in the hall. "I hear you've never smoked pot," she said.

I sighed and replied, "Yes, that's right." Had the entire faculty been informed of my pot inadequacy? Didn't these smart people know it's against the law to smoke pot?

"If you ever decide you want to check it out, just let us know," she said quietly.

"Uh…OK," I said. Now what exactly did that mean? Was she

offering to be my pot dealer? I just stood there in the hall of the high school in total confusion.

When I went home that evening, I shared the happenings of the day with Ed. He had gone to the same high school as I, and was also a *square* when it came to drugs. What was cool in our school was being smart, being a good athlete, going to college, being a cheerleader and even being in the band. After all, our high school band did go to Washington, DC and march in Kennedy's inaugural parade! Our college days were also spent without drugs. *And now I was supposed to feel bad because we didn't smoke pot?* There was something wrong with this picture. I was still fretting.

At the faculty meeting the following week, the principal mentioned we should all be on the lookout for pot smoking at school. I didn't dare open my mouth to say I was so *square* I wouldn't know it if I saw it or recognize it if I smelled it. Again, there was the assumption, and this time from the administration, that all good teachers knew what pot looked like and how it smelled.

After a few more restless nights, I came to a momentous decision. It was my duty as an educator to get familiar with pot so I could recognize it. This didn't come out of a sense of being pressured by my peers, but an honest desire for knowledge. At least that was what I told myself. I mentioned to Betty that if she and Bill just happened to have some pot around that they were going to smoke, perhaps I should observe.

She laughed. "I'll get back to you," she said.

The next week during our lunch period, she flagged me down as we were heading into the cafeteria. "Come with me," she said. We headed for her car in the school parking lot.

"Can we leave campus during lunch?" I asked.

"Don't worry, there's no rule against it," she said as she rolled her eyes.

"Where are we going?" I wanted to know.

"Just a quick little errand around the corner and we'll grab some lunch at the drive-through."

"Ok," I said. I hadn't left the campus during school hours before, but she had been teaching there for two years so I thought she must know the rules.

I climbed in and we headed out of the parking lot. We went three blocks and she pulled into the gas station. I wondered why she had asked me to come along to get gas. This was a full-service station with an attendant, which you don't see anymore. He put a couple of gallons in and came to her window and handed her a plastic bag and she gave him cash.

"See how easy that was?" We pulled out and she rolled up the window.

"Please don't tell me you just bought drugs from that guy," I whispered.

Again she laughed. "All it took was a phone call."

I immediately started looking around for the police. "Why did you do this with me in the car?" I was a little panicked.

"You need to know how easy it is for these kids," she said. "I just wanted you to get the complete picture."

The complete picture was me sliding down in the seat about to wet my pants out of pure fear. I didn't know which emotion was stronger: fear or anger.

"How about a burger for lunch?" She was totally calm and relaxed.

"I think I'll pass. Could you just take me back to school now?" I pleaded in a rather feeble voice. I'm usually a much stronger person and I like to be in control. I knew this had been a mistake. I liked Betty and Bill and they were both exceptionally good teachers. Betty was one of my best friends on the faculty.

We got back to school, she parked in her same spot and I couldn't get out of the car fast enough. "We'll see you tonight about six-thirty," she said as I dashed off.

I had forgotten at that moment I had invited them to dinner. "Sure, fine," I said as I caught my breath. I was so glad to get out of the car and looked around for a lurking undercover law enforcement person on a stakeout to catch teachers leaving the school during lunch to buy pot.

I finished teaching my afternoon classes and headed home to prepare dinner. I couldn't wait to tell my husband what had happened. And then I wondered if that was a good idea. He liked Betty and Bill and what if this changed his mind about them.

They arrived promptly at six-thirty and we had a glass of wine before dinner. After dinner they helped us carry in the dishes to our little kitchen and then we all went into our living room.

"So, did you hear about our big adventure today?" Betty asked my husband.

So much for not telling him about being with her when she bought pot! She relayed the story including my sliding down in the car seat. Ed didn't react too adversely and, in fact, laughed when she demonstrated how I slid down in the seat and covered my head.

"So, we brought the pot, for an educational endeavor," she said as she pulled the plastic bag out of her purse. "But you two need to decide if you want to try it or not. You don't have to, but since you wanted to know what it smelled like, we could light a joint." And with that she pulled out a packet of white, thin papers and put it beside the bag on our coffee table.

I looked at Ed and he looked at me. I guess we were each waiting for the other to make a decision. "Oh, what the hell, why not," he said. I was a little surprised, but I have to admit I was more than a little curious. After all, I was the one who started this whole endeavor.

Betty got out a paper, sprinkled some of the green grassy stuff on it and then rolled it up. She licked the paper so it would stick and twisted the end. Bill lit it for her. She took a long drag and held her breath and then blew it out. She passed it to Bill who did the same thing. They were inhaling and holding the smoke. They asked Ed if he wanted to try some and he did.

"You want to give it a try?" Betty asked me.

Now I needed to explain I had no idea how to smoke…anything. My parents had both been smokers and I vowed when I was about ten years old that I would never take up the nasty habit and I had stuck to that vow.

Ed was trying to quit smoking cigarettes, but had not totally succeeded at this point. He suggested I might want to practice on a Winston from his pack. He went to retrieve it as Betty and Bill finished passing the first joint.

I was trying to figure out how to inhale and that had to be a ridiculous sight. I mostly wanted to blow into the cigarette. After a few tries I sort of got the hang of it and suddenly felt a bit light headed. *Who knew a nonsmoker can get high on a regular cigarette?*

Betty rolled a second joint and they handed it to me. I gave it my best effort and was waiting for some huge wave of "something" to hit me. It didn't. I passed it to my husband. "Do you feel anything?" I asked.

"No, not really," he said.

This passing of the joint went on through a second one and I definitely got to know what pot smelled like. It was an undeniably distinct stink. But I didn't feel anything. No great mellowness, no giggly moments of laughter. Nothing. Ed and I went to the kitchen to serve dessert, leaving Bill and Betty in the living room to finish the last joint she had rolled.

"Did you ever feel anything?" I whispered to Ed.

"No, not really," he answered. "Not my thing."

"Me either," I said.

The bag of pot was not on the table when we went back in to serve dessert. At about ten o'clock, Bill and Betty were saying their good-byes because the next day was a school day. I was ready for the night to be over. So much for that experiment. At least now I knew what it smelled like…and tasted like. Maybe it just took a lot more to get a buzz.

The next day at school Betty winked at me as we passed in hallway. "See you at lunch," she said. I was definitely not going for another car ride with her at lunch!

When I did see her in the lounge, she pulled me aside and said "I need to tell you something. We left you guys the rest of what was in the sack last night."

"You what?" I exclaimed too loudly.

"It was your experiment, so we left it for you in the inside of that statue on your bookcase. If you really want to know how it makes you feel, you should try it again because I'm not sure you ever inhaled last night...and you were being...uh...a little over analytical." *Was analytical just another word for "square?"* She was whispering quietly and for that I was grateful.

"You left that in *my* house? But…but it's illegal." I was mortified.

"It's okay, just don't flush it," she said as she walked away.

I could barely contain myself for my afternoon classes, knowing I had pot in my apartment. I had visions of losing my teacher's license, having to go to court, and being thrown in jail. My "squareness" was in overdrive. Why had I ever let them bring the stuff into our apartment in the first place? I pondered that question as I drove home that afternoon. And I had to admit, I had been curious and the one asking to observe…totally for the sake of gathering information. At least that was my excuse.

As I approached my apartment, I was relieved to not see a police car waiting for me. I knew my imagination was working overtime, but I couldn't wait to get inside to get rid of the illegal drug stuck inside my pretty hollow statue.

Ed wasn't home yet, so there I was, all alone with "It." I pulled the drapes and again peeked out to be sure no police were lurking outside. I pulled out the plastic bag and the packet of papers fell out with it. I couldn't wait to get rid of the illegal marijuana that shouldn't be in my apartment. But what was I going to do with "It?"

Betty had specifically said not to flush it. Would it clog up the plumbing? So if I didn't flush it, how else would I dispose of it? The garbage disposal might clog if the grassy stuff was a plumbing issue. I thought of the trash can, but what if someone found it? I was beginning to panic. I thought of just carrying it outside and scattering it on the grass, but the grass was all covered in snow and it would be easily spotted. I stared at the bag and papers and tried to think clearly.

I had to get rid of this stuff. I couldn't live with the paranoia another day. I started gathering my dirty clothes to take down to the laundry room in the basement of our building while I tried to come up with a good idea. Maybe I could dispose of the bag and papers in a trash can down there. But that might spur an investigation if it was found, and I'm a terrible liar if I get questioned.

I finally made a decision. I took out three papers from the packet by the bag of pot. I laid them out in a line and then I licked them so they would stay together. I poured all of the remaining weed on the papers and rolled a small cigar-sized joint. I licked the papers across the top to seal the joint and then twisted the end as I had seen Betty do it the night before. I struck a kitchen match and lit the thing. The paper at the end flared and I nearly dropped it on the floor. I tried sucking in the smoke, and coughed loudly.

Sitting there all by myself, I was concentrating on how to inhale and I finally seemed to get the hang of it. *Yuck*. It didn't taste good, it made me cough and there was just nothing positive about smoking... anything. Add on top of that the fact that I was breaking the law, and it made the experience totally negative. But I was starting to relax just knowing the pot would soon be out of my possession. I dutifully finished the large joint...because I had to get rid of "It."

Smoking that "pot cigar" took a while. It gave me time to be very philosophical. I had some exceptionally brilliant thoughts, but I don't quite remember the subject of my musing. I was delighted to be finished and suddenly very proud of my ingenious method of disposal. I found myself grinning...a lot. In fact, the whole thing was suddenly very funny and I was laughing out loud.

I gathered my basket and headed down to the laundry room. Suddenly I felt like singing, so an old hymn my Granny used to sing came to mind, *Standing in the Need of Prayer*. I'm not a good singer, but on that afternoon in a New York laundry room I sang like Ella Fitzgerald...or I thought I did. Watching the clothes go around in the dryer was sort of fascinating to me that day, too. *I think I was very lucky no other residents needed to do laundry right then.*

I carried the clean clothes back upstairs, got a snack and opened all the windows for a few minutes to air out the apartment. I would never again have trouble recognizing the smell of pot in the girl's restroom. My educational experiment was over and I was filled with relief and a unique, peaceful calm.

That was the first and last time I ever smoked pot. I had been enlightened, but I was way more comfortable being *square*.

BUTTS AND BEARS
Charlotte Hackman

In the summer of 2016, we took a family day trip from Sugar Mountain, North Carolina to Damascus, Virginia to ride the Virginia Creeper bike trail. It's one of the best bike trails in the country and the easiest, as the section we rode was entirely flat or gently downhill.

There were five of us: myself and my husband Ed, our son Colin and his wife Michelle, and our adorable granddaughter, six-year-old Peyton. After a hearty breakfast we arrived at the bike rental place to pick up our equipment.

I had not ridden a bike for several years, but assumed I could manage. As we got fitted on our bikes, I found they all had hand brakes. *Now that could be a problem.* I would've preferred the old-fashioned pedal brake, and asked the technician if he could disconnect the hand brake from my front wheel.

"Why would you want me to do that ma'am?" he asked with a puzzled look on his young face.

"Well, I suspect it will lesson my chances of me squeezing too hard and throwing myself over the handle bars," I told him.

He looked at my "mature," somewhat overweight body and I know he was thinking it would take a front loader to heft my body over the handle bars. *Not all of us are flat bellied and young!* He suggested I go into the parking area and practice a little bit as he worked with the others.

If I arranged the pedals in just the right position so I could step down on the left one as I took off, I could manage to get started. That wasn't a problem. But stopping was entirely another issue. Trying to squeeze the hand brakes with just the right amount of tension to slow down and get one foot on the ground was a real challenge.

I finally decided we probably wouldn't be stopping very often. I wasn't about to back out of the trip just because I was having trouble dismounting my ride! We loaded all the bikes on a trailer and got in a van that would take us up to the mountain trail, which was built in the bed of an old rail line.

Colin's bike was equipped with a metal bar on his back wheel that connected Peyton's little bike to his. She could pedal, but was attached to the rear of her dad's bike. Michelle looked like she was born to ride. And then there was my husband Ed, who never met a bicycle seat he liked in his adult life…and today was no exception.

I was very carefully getting my left pedal positioned for my "take off" as the others easily got on their bikes and started down the trail. I managed to get on board and thought if I pedaled hard it would steady me because going slow was too much like dealing with the dismount. So I "put the pedal to the metal" and flew past my family like a bat out of hell. *Now that was pretty fun!*

I was getting the hang of riding and feeling pretty confident. Colin and Peyton pulled up beside me as Peyton was laughing and squealing, "We're gonna pass you Mimi!" I pedaled hard but they indeed did pass me, much to Peyton's delight.

I settled into a very comfortable pace and started to enjoy the fantastic scenery along the trail. There were tree branches overhanging the trail, making a tunnel of green. Wild flowers were scattered along the hillside. Ed pulled alongside of me and I was filled with the pure joy of this excursion.

"This damn seat is killing me," he complained. "I'm gonna have blisters on my butt." *Well, so much for the splendid joy.*

"Try alternating your cheeks," I told him. "Or just stand up on your pedals for awhile." He mumbled something that I probably shouldn't repeat, but I did see him attempt to change his position on the seat as we cruised alongside the mountain stream. He moved on ahead of me as I was just enjoying the mountain stream. The water was rushing over large rocks and I could see Colin and Peyton's tandem bike pulled off to the side up ahead.

Now all of my confidence went out the window. *Was I going to have to make a dreaded stop?* I tried slowing down by gently, very gently, squeezing the hand brakes. Maybe I would just ride on past. But as I got closer, I could see there was a beautiful waterfall and Ed had also stopped. *Any excuse to get off that seat.*

Instead of a "running start," I made a "running stop." I nearly crashed into a big tree and then flirted with plunging into the babbling brook. At least it was entertainment for the others as they watched me struggle, and finally manage a wobbly dismount.

We took some pictures and drank some water while Peyton and Colin played in the water. *No splashing!* Michelle caught up and did a graceful dismount, so we waited a little longer for her to enjoy the fun. Ed was happy to be anywhere other than on his seat. I really did feel sorry for him as he was obviously in agony.

Once again, I started my process a little ahead of the others because I had to position my left pedal, and off I went. We rode another hour or so before we came to a small outpost that sold snacks and soda. There were a few other bikers stopped there, sitting around the picnic tables. And once again I was going to have to make my dreaded stop. I might have kept going to avoid the dismount, but nature was calling…loudly.

I actually was coaching myself, *"Slowly, you can do this. Get your foot ready to put down. Squeeze a little harder. Go for it."* I put my foot down, but the bike wanted to keep going and my body got confused. So I took a little rest on the ground, in front of the other bikers. *Humiliating!*

"Are you okay, ma'am? Can we give you a hand?"

"No, no. I'm fine," I said with a forced smile, as I picked my body up and thanked the flat bellied riders. *After all, my mature figure gave me a little extra cushion.*

The rest of my family arrived just as I was getting up and picking up my bike. "Mom, are you hurt?" Colin asked with some concern.

"Nope. Just didn't exactly stick the landing," I tried to joke as I was still brushing the dirt off my butt.

After the potty stop and snacks and a drink, we hit the trail again. Ed asked for about the tenth time, "Are we almost at the end?" His backside was very unhappy.

About twenty minutes down the trail, we crossed an old wooden bridge. There was a man and a boy playing with some snakes and I just zoomed on by. *I could do without wildlife today.*

I was humming as I coasted along the mountain stream. Sunlight was filtering through the trees making patterns on the trail. There was a cool breeze and all was right with the world. I was in the lead with Ed very close behind, followed by Colin and Peyton. Michelle was cruising at her own speed taking in all the glory of her surroundings.

Suddenly, up ahead of me was a looming encounter with wildlife I would never have anticipated. A very large black bear was climbing out of the stream and onto the bike trail several yards directly in front of me!

Oh my God, I'm going to have to stop! Squeeze gently. "Bear, there's a bear up here," I said without shouting too loudly. I wanted to warn my family, but honestly, I was mostly concerned with how I was going to get stopped before I ran into a *big bear*. "Bear up here," I repeated. Ed was already stopped and off his bike, I'm sure, but I didn't have time to look behind me.

The bear stopped, turned, and looked straight at me. *This is not how or when I want to die. Squeeze the brakes. I don't want to fly over the handlebars into him. SQUEEZE the brakes.*

The bear turned back around and quickly lumbered up the slope on the other side of the trail just as I got my bike stopped and my foot on the ground. *My best stop of the day.* Ed pulled up beside me, then Colin and Peyton.

"That was a big-assed bear," Ed exclaimed as he got off his bike.

"Mom, what were you thinking? You were heading right for him! Dang, I couldn't get my camera out fast enough," Colin said with a smile..

"I was about to get eaten by a bear and all you could think about was getting it on film?" I asked him.

"What bear?" shouted Peyton. None of us answered her as we busily started talking at the same time about the size of the bear and my slow stop. "What bear?" she said again, louder.

"There was a big black bear on the bike trail," I said. "Didn't you see him?" I asked.

"Really? Are you joking?" she asked in her sweet and innocent little girl voice.

"No joke," I said.

"Seriously, Pop?" she asked Ed. She knew he wouldn't play a joke on her.

"Honest, Peyton," he said, "and it was a big one."

About that time, Michelle caught up with us and we all started telling her about the bear. She was astonished and not sad about missing the encounter. Then she turned to Peyton and said "Were you scared when you saw the big bear, honey?"

Peyton folded her little arms across her chest sitting there on her bike connected to the back of Colin's bike and with a very pouty face said, "All I saw was Daddy's butt!" We all broke into laughter, which upset her even more.

I was just happy that I had managed to stop without crashing into the bear. We decided that even though the trail was gently downhill, we would all pedal harder for a little bit and stay close together, just in case our bear wanted to visit us again. Happily for us, that was the last we saw of him. Of course, little Peyton hadn't seen him at all and was not pleased to have been stuck behind her dad's behind for the excitement of the day.

We made some new family memories that day on the Virginia Creeper Trail. Ed is not likely to get on another bike seat for a long time, if ever. It took two weeks for his backside to recover. For me, it was a beautiful adventure, spent with my family…and the butts and the bear.

*If you wait for inspiration to write,
you're not a writer; you're a waiter.*
Dan Poynter

MARIE GILLIS is a graduate of Forsyth School for Dental Hygienists, Northeastern University, and the University of Maryland. She is currently a doctoral student at NOVA Southeastern University, majoring in Health Science. Presently, she is self-employed as an educational consultant for accreditation issues, regulatory compliance, and continuing education courses.

She is the author of many scholarly articles, recipient of multiple research grants and awards. She has written textbooks and online courses to prepare for dental hygiene licensing exams.

Marie is pleased to be part of Landfall Writers' Group. As a career scientific writer, she is enjoying writing fiction as a new challenge.

Marie and her husband Chet have made their vacation home in Landfall for four years and are in the process of relocating permanently from Washington, DC. They have four children and two grandchildren. When not writing, Marie enjoys gardening, the beach, and entertaining.

A REVOLUTIONARY FOURTH
Marie Gillis

While we give a modest nod to Philadelphia for the signing of our founding documents, any native Bostonian will tell you that we invented the Fourth of July. It was here, after all, that the Sons of Liberty dumped tea into the harbor to signal the unofficial start of our fight for independence over taxation without representation.

School children in Boston are immersed in the revolutionary history of our country as a rite of passage. We have the home-team advantage and know that it was the Battle of Breed's Hill, not the farther away Bunker Hill in Charlestown, in 1775 that signaled the siege of Boston by the British army.

Many of us can still quote some lines from Longfellow's poem of Paul Revere's ride: "Listen my children and you shall hear of the midnight ride of Paul Revere." The poem depicts the defiance and fearlessness of our fledgling revolutionaries, and yet to be officially called Americans, to rise up against British colonial oppression. One lantern in the bell tower of the Old North Church meant that the British were invading by land, two if by sea. And the answer is.... by sea.

Abigail Adams, one of our founding mothers, started the tradition of celebrating the birth of our nation by serving a poached salmon dinner with egg sauce, peas and new potatoes followed by homemade strawberry shortcake. I can still recall the buttery splendor of my grandmother's biscuits. Most native Bostonians will attest that this is our signature menu and not baked beans, lobster or clam chowder. Abigail was one of the first chefs to approach cuisine with a seasonal flourish; most of these foods are abundant in a July harvest. Perhaps after enduring the sacrifices of war with limited food resources, the fruits from the land and sea celebrated not only independence but the end of war as well. As a child, our extended family would gather at my grandmother's home for this feast on the "night before the Fourth." As a child with a simpler palate than I have today, my favorite part of the meal was the yummy shortcake.

The Freedom Trail is a several-mile tour through our nation's history. If you have never walked its course, then you owe it to yourself to travel to Boston to witness fourteen sites that include the Boston Commons (be sure to take a ride on a swan boat) and the Freedom Tree, where colonial revolutionaries hung the British tax collectors. However, my favorite memories surround one of the stops on the Freedom Trail: the majesty and ceremony involving the USS *Constitution* and the Fourth of July festivities.

The USS *Constitution*, which was named by George Washington, is one of our nation's first battleships. She is moored at U.S. Navy Dry Dock 1 in Charlestown Bay. Most Bostonians can attest to memories of field trips to tour "Old Ironsides" at some point in their elementary school experiences.

Each year on the Fourth of July, she is taken out to the harbor, her sails unfurled in glorious majesty, and she executes a graceful 180-degree turn, fires her canons, and then returns to her slip. This annual rotation alternates her harbor orientation from port to starboard.

I can almost still smell the pungent sulfur and scorched-iron odor from the cloud of smoke that hangs in the air after the canon booms. She is famous for her role in the War of 1812 against the United Kingdom. Hence the reason why a much-adored Bostonian, Arthur Fielder, the late conductor of Boston Pops Orchestra, accompanied the music of the *1812 Overture* with canons and fireworks from the Hatch Memorial Shell on the Esplanade of the Charles in Back Bay every Fourth of July.

We native Bostonians take the Fourth very seriously.

My ideas don't usually come at my desk writing, but in the midst of living.
Anais Nin

John Roper was born in Boston, Massachusetts and lived in Massachusetts, New York, Delaware, Pennsylvania, and California while growing up. The majority of his adult life was spent in Connecticut. He received his undergraduate degree at West Chester University, obtained a Masters degree in world history at the University of Bridgeport and earned thirty credits in radio, television and film at California State University at Fresno and thirty credits in educational computing at Fairfield University .

He taught in the Fairfield Public School system for thirty-nine years and coached boys' and girls' cross country, indoor and outdoor track. In 1981 he was awarded a summer fellowship at Yale University and researched and coauthored *Curriculum Units on Connecticut History* (Yale University Press, New Haven, 1981).

In 2007 he and his wife retired to Wilmington, North Carolina. He has two sons, one of whom lives in Chicago, the other in New Jersey. He has done volunteer work for the University of North Carolina at Wilmington track team, the Cameron Museum, local road races, and a yoga studio.

He began writing in 2014 as therapy following the death of his wife and enjoys the support, camaraderie, and constructive suggestions of the Landfall Writers' Group. John is currently working on a fictional novel of a young woman's life experiences.

HGTV
John Roper

After losing my wife following a brutally grueling seven year battle with stage IV renal carcinoma, I was emotionally exhausted. I did not want to watch anything on TV that was sad, depressing, or upsetting so I found myself frequently watching HGTV (Home and Garden Television) shows. Why would a sixty-eight-year-old man suddenly find home improvement shows so appealing? Because they always have a happy ending. People appear on the shows with hopes and aspirations of achieving their dream home. Designers take them through renovations, and without fail people are thrilled with their new kitchens, family rooms, bathrooms, master bedrooms and so forth.

However, there is some predictability to the shows. *The Property Brothers* always show a perfect house to the purchasing couple that is well out of their price range. When Drew informs them that they can't afford the house, they are shocked. "Why did you show us a house we can't afford?" His answer is always, "We can give you everything you want in a house. You'll just have to buy one that's not in good shape at a cheaper price, and we'll fix it up." Usually at least one of them will protest that he/she doesn't want to do a renovation. Why are they shocked at the prospect of renovation? Don't these people watch the show in advance? It's a show where people buy dilapidated homes and renovate them into dream homes.

On *Love It or List It,* the one half of the couple who doesn't want to move will find fault with every home that David shows them until the last one which they will both like very much. During the renovation of the existing home, Hillary will almost always bump into serious structural, electrical, plumbing, or asbestos problems that must be addressed, making it impossible for her to do one or more of the planned renovation items on their list. The person who wants to move will trash Hillary about not delivering what they wanted. But Hillary will work her magic, and despite setbacks, the house will look beautiful. When Hillary and David ask, "Will you love it or list it?" The couple will answer, "This is a lot harder than we thought it would be."

On *Fixer-Upper,* Joanna Gaines seems to have a knack for finding junk on the side of the road. Somehow she will be able to take an old gate with tetanus-ridden rusty hinges and peeling lead paint, have her husband Chip nail it to a wall, and the couple will be as taken with it as if it were an Andrew Wyeth original.

On the show *Flip or Flop,* Tarek el Moussa is always firmly convinced that they will be able to renovate a house at a price that is usually 50-100 percent less than what it will actually cost by the end of the renovation. His wife, Christina, will argue for upgrades. He will be opposed to every upgrade as too costly. She will insist that the upgrade will improve their chances for a sale. He will puff his cheeks and his eyes will bulge with every expensive addition that she suggests. In the end she is almost always right, and they sell the house for a handsome profit

However, the most predictable aspect about all the HGTV shows is that at the reveal, the couple will walk in and at least one wide-eyed, exuberant homeowner will exclaim, "Oh my goodness! This is... *amazing*. These floors are... *amazing*. This counter is... *amazing*. This backsplash is... *amazing*." The homeowners seem to be so overwhelmed with how wonderful their renovation is that they have suddenly become devoid of adjectives - with the exception of "amazing" and the occasional "awesome." If there was a drinking game where one would take a drink every time the word "amazing" was said on these shows, viewers would be plastered by the end. The word "amazing" should be reserved for things that are truly amazing, such as the birth of a child, winning twenty-three Olympic gold medals, the atomic bomb or the Resurrection. But subway tile? Laminate flooring? Glass tile? "*Amazing!*" Really?

Below is a list of adjectives I would like to be distributed to those appearing on HGTV shows so that they can expand their vocabulary:

Superb	Captivating
Wonderful	Magnificent
Terrific	Hypnotic
Fantastic	Excellent
Exceptional	Eye-catching
Beautifully crafted	Radiant
Captivating	Charming
Magnificent	Outrageous
Hypnotic	Gorgeous

Excellent	Extraordinary
Beautiful	Radiant
Astonishing	Charming
Remarkable	Nice (as in, "pretty nice," "very nice" and "really nice")

Hopefully, at the end of the show, ecstatic homeowners could refer to this list, and for once we could avoid hearing the word "amazing". Instead, we might hear, "This kitchen is marvelous!" "The family room is *wonderful*." "These built-ins are beautifully crafted." If this were to happen, it would truly be A… MA…jor refreshing change.

Time to find another house to renovate.

Write hard and clear out what hurts.
Ernest Hemingway

Myrna L. Brown lived and worked in Burkina Faso, French West Africa for seven years. Her experience there reinforced her commitment to promoting positive change for women and children.

For the past three years, Myrna has served on the Project Grants Committee of Virginia Gildersleeve International Fund (VGIF). During that period, the VGIF process for making grants has undergone a dramatic transformation. She currently serves on the VGIF Board as Vice President for Strategic Planning.

Fulfilling a lifetime dream, Myrna made a career transition to healthcare in the 1990s. After achieving her RN credentials, she has worked as a floor nurse in a large metropolitan hospital and later as a nurse in a hospice care practice. She has a particular knack for seeing opportunity and understanding how to harness it for positive organizational change and growth. Myrna is the mother of three daughters.

Myrna has published two novels: *Of Unseen Things Above* and *A Season of Mists*. Both have received very positive reviews. She is currently working on her third novel.

A BOY'S BEST FRIEND
Myrna Brown

The edge of the forest the brothers walked through was thick with underbrush past their ankles. If not for the paths the boys had tramped into the rich black soil, they wouldn't have been able to see a way through the bramble of blackberry briars, thistles, sword ferns or even through the thick of the trees of southwest Washington.

They stopped to eat the clover, pulling each perfect leaf from its stem, puckering. The salmon berries were just hard green knots on the bushes.

Limping beside them was Punky, their Springer Spaniel, who sniffed about and half-heartedly flushed birds from the huckleberry bushes. There was a sudden fluttering and rush of wings as the small birds abandoned the red berries and settled obscurely in the tall timber. Punky plopped down on the trail with his chin on his paws. He whimpered, but the boys didn't hear him.

It was Christmas time and the boys were in the woods looking for the best tree. The younger followed the older as they walked on the path they had marked as Eagle Nest, going beyond the foyer of thick brush that hid the forest. Now the tips of the hemlocks waved like flags and the cedars' branches, swept by the breeze, were reminiscent of a court of royalty bowing, draping gracefully, nearly touching the ground.

The older boy tucked into a hollow stump and pretended he was a king, using a stick for a scepter and woven twigs for a crown. The younger knelt, stretched his arms and offered both hands full of clover. Again, Punky rested. He raised himself and hobbled with effort when they whistled. They couldn't remember a time without Punky beside them. Since birth he had been their companion, their scout, their protector; constant in his attention to them.

Punky's habit was to wait in the driveway to greet their father when he came home from work at four o'clock. Punky could tell time, they always said. True to form, he stopped in front of the boys, barked and turned away, heading home. When they called him, he sat momentarily in the path and looked back at them, as if deciding what to do. He barked twice and left the boys to return to sit in the driveway, nose pointed toward the road, looking for the Public Utilities' line truck to pull in.

In the woods, the boys came upon an occasional deciduous alder, bare leafed, its stark branches stiff and inflexible in the breeze. Springing up in the slightest shaft of sunlight, the alders were invasive and poached the light, but the young evergreen timber over time overtook them. Slim and leafless until spring, the alders provided the boys with their cones - strobilus - shaped like small lanterns that hung all winter. As was their habit, the boys threw them at a nearby tree, listening for the sharp whack. The cones often provided ammunition for an afternoon of practicing their aim. The young one's arm was shorter and not as strong, and he consistently aimed high. But remembering their mission, they went back to searching.

The boys went deeper into the woods. Leaving far behind the underbrush that caught and tangled in their pant legs, they walked under the canopy of the forest and far past the end of their Eagle Nest trail leading east.

They came upon a spongy floor of moss expanding at least an acre. Wooded with evergreen, it was swept clean but for the fir cones and litter of broken branches, like a modern, wall-to-wall rug. It even crept over the fallen trees the boys had to hoist themselves over in their quest for a Christmas tree.

An artist might struggle to capture the lush green tones in the breadth of the moss as it flowed like a riverbed as far as the boys could see. Encountering the unblemished soul of the forest, they stood for a moment, perceiving somewhere in their innocence that it was a privilege to come upon such mysterious beauty. There was a rhythm to the dripping from a recent rain.

The boys stopped to count the rings of a freshly blown-down tree, and they knew by marking each hundredth ring that some were hundreds of years old. They couldn't imagine a time so long ago. Their sense of history included stories of the Old West, cowboys and Indians, good guys, bad guys, and certainly Superman, but it didn't go much farther back than when the old orchard had been planted, for instance.

They knew that the flat tails of the beaver damming a nearby creek were used for hats in the olden days. They knew the settlers had worn them. Their father could tell them of the days of horses and buggies, but they only knew firsthand about Fords and Chevys.

There were war stories from Europe seeping through, leaking upon children and stirring their imaginations about playing war. Their father had been called up but then deferred. A green army cot was folded away, and they used the blanket of the same military green for picnics.

If the brothers were to lie down and look up, they would have become happily dizzy as the trees wheeled in slow circles, but they hurried realizing the twilight was deepening,

For all the magic of the forest, it can also play tricks on you about time. Even though the days are short in the winter, sunsets over the Columbia River dally and saturate the sky, prolonged like the slow drawing of a velvet curtain. In a meadow the colors can stretch into an elongated sky and just at twilight into darkening tones of purple and orange, like an injury that has become a spreading bruise. But deep into the forest, the dark of day comes more quickly, quenching even the light of the stars.

They walked circles around among the new growth, the offspring of a large spruce or a towering Douglas fir, always looking for what to their eyes was the straightest and most beautifully shaped.

The one the brothers found was about two miles east of home. It was much taller than they, just as they wished. Small, moving puddles of evening light still leaked through the canopy of trees. Briefly, they played hopscotch on them. The sky closed in less than a minute. Looking up from their feet on a moonless night, they went back to their task to chop down the tree.

Like other trees they'd found, having been given this responsibility before, it lacked branches on one side. They came to an agreement that their father could drill holes and attach new ones. He had done it before, and they could use lots of strands of silver tinsel to hide the remaining bare spots. The older cut it close to the ground in order to keep branches.

They imagined it all decorated even after the light slid away. The younger wanted to find an army jeep out of the Sears and Roebuck catalogue beneath the tree. The older wanted a Swiss Army knife.

The sound of their hatchet cutting a wedge into one side of the tree was smothered, without echo, absorbed in the forest before the shocks could resound. Finally the tree thrashed and fell with a rush and thump, a young spruce with strong limbs to hold ornaments. They knew to jump back. In the seeming silence one could hear the soughing of the trees and the last harsh calls of a blue jay. Tick, tick, tick went the dripping trees.

Deer came out to graze and peered at the boys as they began dragging the tree, disturbing the rug of moss and startling the beetles beneath. The beetles scurried back for the dark center of their universe, which seemed blacker in the descending night as there was no shine from their backs.

The Christmas tree swept a new path behind them but they didn't find their old path. So far their way home swerved and circled upon itself as they searched for the way they had come. The boys looked around as best they could in the darkness that enveloped them. The older stopped and swallowed. He said, "Let's find the trees we marked."

They had known to mark their way after they broke away from Eagle Nest trail. With their pocket knives they had slit and peeled away the bark of a few Cascara trees, exposing the trunk, a shiny wet surface, cool and sticky to touch. They had carved arrows pointing home as they went. On their return, they expected to have the light of day and it should be easy enough to find them, it seemed to them. They had piled up the stripped bark to collect later because they sold it in gunny bags after it dried, and they were told it was used for heart medicine. With their earnings they bought funny books, comics with cops and robbers, super heroes like Clark Kent. Lois was just a girl and couldn't do what Clark did.

The boys felt their way in the dark; they embraced the trees and searched with their hands for the wet trunks of the cascara they had marked and scuffed their feet to find the peeled bark beneath. They continued one direction and then another. The birds were quiet. They heard the "who-who" of a spotted owl. The younger boy's shoulders slumped as he lifted the tip of the tree.

They heard a rustle in the brush alongside them. Some creature slipped away, breaking branches, perhaps more deer or a bear. Bears didn't always hibernate this early into winter. They didn't know the habits of bears at night.

The boys' home and the acre it sat on were on the edge of the forest, and if not for the shiny leaved rhododendrons that bounded it, it would have seemed like an incidental meadow like the one that surrounded the gnarly old orchard across the road. The virgin forest around the house had never before been logged. Never had a caterpillar's wide tracks overrun the vegetation beneath the stand of evergreens. The ground didn't have the telltale heaps and piles a gyppo logger would have left. Even a small dozer would have roughened the ground, and the scars would have remained for years to come. And so it remained pristine, like nearly everything around them. Their father worked hard but he had called their life in the Elochoman Valley "The Life of Riley," that is, before their mother boarded the train to Topeka.

That night, lost in the dark, the younger stayed the tree's length behind his brother, stopping and starting when he did. They wore red plaid-wool jackets, which may as well have been black, so deep the darkness had become.

Like the virgin forest, the house, too, where the father waited, was pristine, nearly finished finally by the father with white slate shingles as siding and a cedar roof. Their father had split his own roof shingles.

In contrast, the shingles on the outhouse soon to be dismantled were thin, gray and weathered. The privy seemed to have been there since time began and stood somewhat crookedly behind the house. Sometimes they threw rocks at it, but the younger one couldn't hit the broad side of a barn.

The third building was the pump house for the well the father had dug. The shakes were still bright and wet looking, so recently had it been built. When digging the well, the boys had carried the passed-along buckets of wet red clay to dump on the edge of the property. An old white-bearded friend in bib overalls had witched the spot, dousing with his L-shaped divining rod, and the first attempt at digging was a success. The boys handled the douser, smoothened by years of use.
No more hauling water for indoor use; it now came right into the kitchen. Finally, their father could build the pink-tiled bathroom their mother had wanted for so long. After the water heater was

installed there would be spigots for hot and cold and a bathtub. As it was, since babies, the boys were bathed in a tin wash tub. They barely fit anymore.

This was the only home they had known. Their mother, whom they had witnessed crying at times, her face reflected in the dark window she faced when she washed the dishes, went back to Kansas to live, leaving the wet, moldy northwest. Now it was the boys who washed, dried and put away the dishes. The skillet was the hardest and they took turns scrubbing it with a Brillo pad.

After she was gone, they began standing instead of sitting in the wash tub and scrubbed themselves. The older poured water over the younger's head to rinse him, and they laughed. The younger couldn't reach to the top of his brother's head. Their mother's absence was strongest then and at supper time and while they cleaned up. No one spoke of her, not even at bedtime when their father read *The Hardy Boys* to them.

Everything around their home had been started from almost nothing, except for the initial small investment in the rural acre of land that allowed for a deep and wide yard. They had begun with the shell of an old cabin with a stone fireplace intact, the outhouse in back. Until the add-on, the boys had slept in bunk beds near their parents, the oldest on the bottom.

In the yard a Firestone tire hung on a cedar, and it cleared any of the tall cedars' branches when one of the brothers pushed the other into the sky of unfolding clouds, gray upon gray, gray upon white, gray upon blue.

To build the sidewalk of salvaged red brick stretching from the road to the door, the boys had carried the bricks in an old wheelbarrow bought second hand. Sometime their father would knock off the old used grout with his hammer, but for the most part, the bricks were rough and speckled the color of an old setting hen. The walk was perfectly straight. Their father had worked on his knees pushing the fresh grout with his trowel.

Punky, before his accident, had taken turns being with the father and following the boys back and forth, panting, tongue dripping. He scrubbed his tail against the grass back and forth and when he stood, it was already wagging. Punky had gone to the garage and brought the father's leather gloves, but they weren't needed. The boys worked in cadence with their father and there were few words.

"Good boy," their father said to Punky when he dropped the chamois-colored raw-leather gloves near him. The boys had gloves but they weren't of raw hide. They were worsted wool and they were wearing them when they were trying to find their way home, in fact. Their mother had attached them to a cord so they wouldn't forget or lose them.

When the father bucked firewood, the boys loaded the trailer in neat stacks and never spoke over the noise of the chain saw. Various hand motions or the thrust of their father's jaw communicated what he wanted. When the father cut the motor, the silence of the forest hung among them, like a significant moment.

The splitting of the larger pieces took longer and the boys took turns picking them up, fitting the wedges together in the trailer. Their hands smelled of pitch, even when they removed their gloves. Punky sat in the tractor seat. Sometimes the father stood and stretched his back, breaking the rhythm of their work. Ever present, Punky would stir, turn and resettle.

Punky hopped alongside the truck to welcome the father. As his master removed his caulked boots, loosening and flicking aside their leather laces, Punky licked the thick waterproofed toes darkened with creosote. After the boots were pulled off, and as he was being petted and talked to, Punky slumped at the father's feet.

The boys' father moved the recliner all the way back then straight, then forward. He drummed his fingers against the oak armrest. He put down his newspaper and tilted his head toward the back door now and then over the course of an hour or more. He smoked several cigarettes one after the other. He listened for the shuffle they would make removing their boots and hats, wrestling out of their jackets. It was dark and no light edged the blue draperies hanging in front of the new picture window.

Punky, who sat beside his feet, began to pace, as did he. They went from the kitchen to the back door and back to the living room. Punky whined at the door. One could hear the uneven clicking of his three paws on the black-and-white linoleum their father had laid in the kitchen. Otherwise, it was quiet. Finally, near the door, Punky barked. Because of Punky's injuries, the father had wanted to spare him from searching the woods.

"Go find them, good boy," their father finally said, lightly patting Punky's unwounded side as he opened the door. He stepped out into the moonless night and called their names, knowing they couldn't hear him unless they were close enough to be safely on one of their own paths. The paths began as one but branched out in several directions. The boys had painted the names with the direction they went in parentheses. The pieces of bark were attached to a post their father had set in the ground with a handheld post-hole digger.

He swept the flashlight over the edge of the forest catching the signs. He remained standing in the cooling night while Punky went after the boys.

When Punky was struck by the yellow, county dump truck as he crossed the road, he was left in the ditch, the same ditch where the boys caught tadpoles in the small ponds of their palms, where they waited for the miracle of the little green frogs. The ditch was pink with Punky's blood as it trickled downstream. They had carried him to the kitchen, bleeding especially from his right side, and it was several weeks before he could lift himself up from the kitchen floor. Their mother had cried then, too and she held the water very near Punky's nose and made soothing noises. They sopped up his blood into the good white towels. For several days until the blood soaked out, they all had to share the same towel.

Punky now had three legs, the fourth having been amputated by the father as the boys held him down. The nearest veterinarian was at least fifty miles away. They had wiped their noses with their t-shirts, holding their trembling pet while their father worked the hand saw through the bone. Now Punky lay down often and wasn't eating well. Too painful to use, it still bled when he scraped the stub accidentally.

In the darkened woods, the boys found other cascara trees but not the ones they had skinned. They drew a circle, exploring fifty steps out and back, single file. They moved and drew another circle. Finally, they decided to stay put.

Beneath the hollow of a downed tree, they agreed to pray to be found. Perhaps Punky wasn't too tired to come. Nearly inside the rotted stump, the younger knelt and prayed. Getting up off his knees, he helped the older build a moss-covered bed. They placed the Christmas tree near their heads as a kind of wall for protection. When the younger of the two fell asleep, the older took off his jacket and placed it around his brother's legs. He kept the hatchet near. At daylight, he would know east from west. It was the Eagle Nest trail they needed to find. He too drifted into sleep with his arm around his brother.

When Punky found the boys, after sniffing up one path and down another, he stood for a moment, just looking on. Then he burrowed his way under the branches of the just-found Christmas tree. Panting, he pushed his nose into the face of the dozing older boy and whined in his ear. He was winded and wet with perspiration. Still, he had run in his own fashion, now laying down heavily next to the youngest who continued to sleep.

The older boy embraced Punky and buried his face in the white fur around his neck. He stroked his nose. He let some time go by so the younger boy and the dog could rest before he roused them. He bound the dog's raw right stump with a sleeve torn from his tee shirt. He took back his jacket.

They went single file, the older dragging the tree behind him, the younger following while attempting to lighten the load by lifting the top of the tree from the ground. They were led by their oldest friend,

Punky, who hobbled home without stopping.

Their father stood at the head of the trail. They saw him by the brief red tip of his cigarette. He rewarded Punky with what was to be their supper: nearly a half pound of ground beef. Punky turned it down but he drank and drank.

Under the single bulb of the garage, their father nailed together two pieces of a two-by-four and stood the tree that was slightly crooked. Taking it down, he tapered the bottom of the trunk in an effort to straighten it when it sat into the stand. He drilled holes for the branches they cut from the lower part of the tree to insert them closer to the middle where it was most bare. Once inside, it went in front of the new picture window.

Even though they had hurried the search, it was now a handsome tree. The boys were into the boxes, pulling out the strings of colored lights, making sure they worked. They had to try them, one at a time until they found the one that prevented the whole string from lighting up. They had a pattern to vary the colors so red wasn't beside red and green wasn't next to green. The younger one handed his brother each bulb to try. The wrinkled bows were lined up in a row of varying sizes, some predating their birth. Some of the glass ornaments had broken. They lined the good ones up by color. There were pinecones from eastern Washington. The tinsel was stretched to its full length on the rug ready to be hung. They would hang extra where the tree was still somewhat bare. They turned the tree so they only saw the best side.

The phone rang. 110J5 had three long rings. They waited for the third long ring. The older was allowed, and he picked it up. Elsie, the operator, said, "Long distance calling."

"It's long distance," the younger one called to his father.

"I've left Topeka, and I'll be home for Christmas," their mother said to their father. Her father had recommended she come home and bought her a ticket, through Denver, out to Portland. The older turned the egg timer upside down so they wouldn't go over the three minutes. They stood nearby as their father talked, his voice softening, holding the mouthpiece close.

They told Punky their mother was coming home and rubbed his ears. Punky settled beneath the tree being decorated, sighed deeply, and his last dream may have been about the joys of Christmas. Their mother was probably in the dream, and the drapes were probably opened so everyone going by could see the lights from outside. Surely, they were there all together.

The boys dug his grave that night near the edge of the forest, left of the Eagle Nest trail, and the younger sniffled as they buried him with only the flashlight to see. Their shovels sliced into the moist soil almost silently. Their father pounded a cross made of leftover lumber into the ground. The Christmas lights from the picture window were reflected on the cross.

They stood and the younger grabbed the pant leg of his father. The older turned his back and walked away.

FAMILY TIES
Myrna Brown

The untended cabin, the old man's nearly one-room home, held itself together at the end of a curbed and sidewalked street that abruptly became his driveway. Until you reached his one-way dirt road, you wouldn't realize a house sat back there beneath those tall, sprawling oak trees on wonderful property, nearly two acres, "dirt," on which to build. It was any contractor's dream. In Annandale, Virginia, it was worth a handsome amount, enough to turn one's life upside down.

As for him, the old man had held out. The developers building three-story homes tried to get the city involved. But he had always lived there and wanted to stay. His youngest son pounded several *No Trespassing signs* in the ground, which hung crookedly. Weeds, responding to the season and recent rains, snaked up and curled about as if their tentacles were purposeful, intended to add character.

He simply refused to move even though he knew his ending was at hand. Never mind the doctors; he knew somewhere in his gut before seeing them that his time had come.

Large branches fell and stayed where they had fallen, even across the roof. All the leaves that had ever dropped were matted deeply together and the yard was interminably brown, almost boggy from all the snow of the winter that was now suddenly spring. Healthy young Dogwoods developed roots between and beneath, and their stratified blossoms fell and dusted the earth.

There was a pristine beauty to the unmanaged property that a developer wouldn't have achieved. The trees shadowed the roof, which over time came to match the slick brown of the yard. Patches on the roof revealed the tarpaper, and some of the shingles were slipping out of their intended pattern. But a certain beauty prevailed, like one might see in a passing, unusually shaped cloud.

Inside, he sat all alone, as he had over time, in the same brown rocker, rickety now. He had reared four children here. They were considered Black/African American even though their mother was a Native American. There wasn't a suitable category for their mix of genes, and he told the census workers who came from time to time that it was none of their business. They always left in a huff just like the social worker the county had assigned to him.

She was a hippy, plump woman not at all his style, and she talked to him like she might talk to a child or someone demented and hard of hearing. He preferred women who were tall and stately, the very ones who nearly always turned him down. Except for Lizette. She actually loved him, he believed, even to this day.

Everyone was looking out for his interests but him. Lizette hadn't back then. She left him when the girls went into puberty one after the other and were too much to handle unless she had more *help* from him. They grew up and went through college in spite of how their mother had given up on them and how their parents had disagreed about their upbringing. He *gave in* to them she said. She left him to do it by himself and didn't show up again until she became fed up with alcohol-soused residents of the reservation and came home again. She was the one who gave in to the boys.

The Fairfax County Schools had done their job, but the boys went adrift anyway. They were younger and he had expected them to track just like their older sisters. He would have whipped them but Liz had seen enough of that kind of parenting on the reservation and held him back.

Liz was still in the area and dropped in to see him now and again, more often now that he was sick, even though they hadn't coped well together. Maybe the house was too small, but now in their older years, they abided each other; more, they cherished one another quietly, without blame.

Occasionally she hauled in a case of everyday-the-same red-and-white cans of condensed chicken noodle soup and two every-day-the-same yellow boxes of Cheerios®, and he was set for up to three weeks. He used Carnation® powdered milk and the box sat on the counter near the old electric stove with three coiled black burners. The back burner had been pulled out and it left a black hole. Dried cheerios sometimes spilled and collected there.

For breakfast and dinner, he needed only two bowls. After he finished, he rinsed them and left them in the sink with two pitted and tarnished silver-plated spoons puddled in water.

He was small and not very tall. His features were hard to describe, but he looked resolute in his expression as if he had a personal goal he determined to achieve and was getting there. Some might have seen as a stubborn look. His coarse hair was like leftover metal filings. His nose was pugged and he kept a handkerchief in his chair so he didn't have to get up if it ran. Usually after the Cheerios®, it ran.

Liz said to stop eating them, but they were his favorite and he didn't change his ways for anybody, sometimes to his detriment. Somewhere along the line he had decided he didn't want advice - about anything.

If he changed clothes it was at his daughters' insistence. They brought fresh sheets and took away his wash that, when returned, sat in a cardboard box not far from the wood stove. Every day he threw what he wore in on top, and they had to sort it when they came, the dirty from the clean.

He kept himself clean; no one had to insist on that. He washed up with a green bar of Palmolive soap at the kitchen sink twice a day, just after his Cheerios® and before he went to his bed. He had a pink, scratched plastic dish tub just for that purpose. It sat beneath the open space beneath the sink on a wooden crate.

Otherwise, he stayed in his chair and the gold cushion on the rocker seat was flattened and shaped to his body. A new red one lay on the two-person sofa, and the cat - named Ruby by the girls - had taken to it. Ruby curled into its space until he called it to have leftover

Cheerios® or what was left of the chicken noodle soup. They only ate twice a day.

There were four children and it was his two daughters who took him to the doctor when he was in obvious pain with the damned stomach problems. He refused chemotherapy and radiation and was told he had some weeks or perhaps months left. He took it all in and wanted to be left in peace to sit in his rocker near the stove. How to set about going eluded him but it didn't change his consistent expression. Life came at you, and you couldn't dodge it.

As it turned out, the daughters believed he needed extra care, someone to check in and make sure he was able to make the step down to the added-on bathroom and the kitchen. When they went to obtain hospice services through the federal provision everyone has available to them, they didn't expect to get a team of people seeing to him.

First the admittance nurse came. She was the person he would be assigned to and luckily, he took to her or it may have all gone awry. When she took his vitals, her body was close and warm and he remembered Lizette in her youth, the tall and beautiful Native American he still loved and who birthed his children. *Years pass*, he thought in those minutes as the nurse examined him, *and you don't know the value of what you have in the moment; only later do you know what you should have cherished or thrown in the burn barrel.* He hadn't argued back then when they were family, but he probably should have, he now thought. If he hadn't stood his ground then, he would now.

A chaplain came, but his views seemed to the old man to be conveyed in an aggressive and ambiguous manner. He didn't quote the Bible like a Baptist minister might. The old man wasn't anointed with oil and prayed over like a Holy Roller might have done. No Roman Catholic cross hung from his neck. He was vaporous and not distinguished. Khaki pants, an open collar. He didn't even wear socks.

When the social worker came, she seemed to have the same toneless voice as the chaplain. (It was her habit to keep a straight face even when others lost it.) Plus, she seemed nosy to him. He was tired of people coming through his door.

The aide was refused outright. Only the nurse had connected and communicated with the old and sick and tired man. When the nurses, aides, social workers and chaplain all convened in the office with a single doctor for report at the end of the day, they all told him that the old man hadn't accepted their services, neither spiritually nor mentally, and he was adamantly opposed to anyone who wanted to bathe him. The doctor had fifty or so patients and didn't wrestle with anything much except for new prescriptions and big changes in the vitals. He increased the morphine for one patient and stepped up the number of days they visited another patient. But the old man's blood pressure ranged from 140-170, which was pretty good for someone older who would take no medications.

Thus, he was left alone except for the nurse. She came twice a week rather than once. She wore white; only white. Even then he asked about her hat. How could you tell one from the other?

She came on her own time sometimes in the evening after she had finished with charts and paperwork. He knew, because she told him, that he would have to move to the basement of one of his daughter's homes. But he wouldn't consent.

The daughters who came to see the nurse before he was admitted said he had sworn not to leave his home. Now he was even more insistent, they said. The nurse who herself was tall and had gentle, smile-wrinkled features said in time he would come to terms with receiving care.

He wasn't safe, and hospice care couldn't by law leave him in his home alone. Would the daughters be willing to stay with him? Both said they couldn't give up their teaching positions. Who would care for their children? They couldn't afford to hire anyone. Besides, in the old cabin, only one bedroom was furnished. Someone would have to sit in a chair all night with him and that would have to be brought in. There were no beds available in the surrounding facilities, the social worker reported.

The nurse met with the son who lived locally. He was a welder, as his father had been. However, he told how he wouldn't be able to put his two children through college with the hourly wage he was receiving. He couldn't afford to take the time off to sit with his father; someone else would swoop up his job. He was already in the hole: there were no benefits and no pension; he had drained his 401K.

The nurse listened, knowing it would be up to her to persuade the old man - a tired man, literally at the end of the road - to leave his home.

Therefore, the daughters took him to Doctor Richards, the oncologist, and after the appointment, did not deliver him home to his rocking chair in the little house at the end of the road. According to plan, the nurse met them at the oldest daughter's home and attempted to sooth him as she showed him his new quarters: a room in the basement with a modern bathroom without the rusty sink and the constant drip. The toilet didn't run and had a lid. The tank filled and that was that. He would come to miss the soothing sounds of a running toilet. He had a well. So what?

They had ordered a hospital bed. It was lowered electronically to its lowest level. Initially he balked, but there within grasp was the afghan he used daily, and he proceeded to straighten it on the bed that would be his. Even he knew he was truly tired after being examined and questioned. So he rested there and everyone crossed their fingers that he would comply when he wakened.

The son brought Ruby. Ruby seemed at home. She rubbed against the leg of the nurse. Evie, the nurse manager, picked her up and lifted her to the bed and deposited her against the wall, near the old man's hand. He slipped his hand under her belly and pulled the cat to his chest. He slipped off his shoes by pushing his toes against his heels, and they fell beside the bed. The cat nestled and lay its head down, almost as if it were listening to the beat of his heart. He relaxed and was purred into sleep by the tiny vibrations he felt on his chest.

He would ask almost daily that he be taken to the cabin as he picked up Ruby and sat rocking slowly, sometimes dozing. The oldest daughter would wait to respond. "There's no food in the house," she would say when evening came. They had removed the tins and boxes except for the coffee. There's one last cup he'd say.

But the old man didn't die even after three months. He came to know his daughters' children, some of whom were long legged and fine featured like Lizette. The youngest had his nose, but the high cheek bones of Lizette.

From his bed he used the cushion brought from the rocker to prop himself. Christina, who was ten, sometimes read to him until he fell asleep. In spite of his poor teeth, he ate a variety of food. The meatloaf was like his mother's. Life opened up to him in the company of others. He listened keenly to what was going on upstairs. He knew their schedules and waited for their sounds. They came one by one, even the son-in-law, who smelled like wood shavings.

When time to report, the nurse talked of how the old man lingered and even improved. The cancer was stripping him of strength and the scale trended down when Evie weighed him in a sling they brought to move him to a chair.

Everyone in report, even the rather disconnected doctor, concurred that sometimes people hold off from dying because there's one more thing they want, someone they wish to talk to or something symbolic like reviewing of pictures or one last birthday.

They tried to ease him through but he stayed on, more often in pain than not. Evie puzzled over the old man, as did his children. He refused his medications and withstood the gripping pain in his belly. They had a *comfort pack* provided by hospice in the refrigerator to give him medicine should he ask, but the morphine stayed wrapped in its tiny packets and the Fentanyl patches remained intact. He didn't want to be stuck, so there was no intravenous drip.

Talking to her eight-year-old daughter Missy at bedtime, the mom asked if she remembered when they called her other grandfather and he asked to speak to her just the day before he died.

Her other grandfather loved to tell stories, some made up, some true, but always with a wonderful twist at the end. On the phone, very sedated, he began another: "Once upon a time…," but he hadn't gone on.

Missy had grieved as she would again even while she swung in the tall swing the other grandfather had built for her with the reddish leather suede seat. But she had memories pressing in on her mind that consoled her, mostly, until sometimes at bedtime. She was already eight back then. For sure she remembered. Her grandfather never remembered where he left off with the story, but she knew he already knew the ending; she just didn't get to hear it. Someday in the future she would take up her pen and paper and write stories that would knock the socks off her teachers and finally readers who should know a good story when they heard it.

The nurse didn't sleep well one night. About 3:00 AM she awoke, startled. She was accustomed to her husband's snoring. It wasn't that. Three of the old man's children had come to their father's bedside. Where was the fourth child? Why hadn't he been called to come to the bed side? The oldest boy should know his place in a family. But no one spoke of him.

"Rodney is in prison," the daughters said the next day, "in federal prison out in California." The nurse asked if they could call him. "It's not allowed," they said. "It was a violent crime." He hadn't spoken with any family in over two years.

The nurse spoke to person after person and somewhere in the administrative chain of the prison, someone said the son could call his father.

When the time came, the old man said "My son, my son." The time of the call was limited and when the time was up, the phone disconnected. He released the phone to Liz and she put it softly in its cradle. She straightened the afghan and patted his leg.

That afternoon the nurse could see he was in the end stages of dying. His breathing changed from sixteen breaths a minute to nine or ten. He sighed and they were drawn out, like the air going out of a deflating tire.

His three local children stood by waiting. Evie might have called for a suction machine to come from the office, but he was ready now, she could tell.

The old man entreated the absent angel to come, and the presence came as the children hovered. He passed gently, and in that moment, it was as if he accompanied the breathless spirit as it sprinted through the slatted basement window and escaped this world.

Don't tell me the moon is shining,
show me the glint of light on
the broken glass.
Anton Chekhov

Sarah Giachino was raised in Spencer, West Virginia and is the youngest - and only daughter- of four children. Her father, Charles O. Hardman, USA 117th INF 30 DIV, and her mother Mary endured a twenty-month separation during WWll. All of her life, Sarah listened to her dad's recollections of his combat experience and understood his deep commitment to sharing his memories with her family and their community. She returned with her parents and family on several trips to the many battlefields and American cemeteries of Europe, retracing his war route while keeping a diary.

Early in 2001, she discovered twenty months of consecutive love letters written between her parents in their family home attic and realized the importance of their correspondence. In these letters, her father mentions the visits from the traveling USO Show Troop-Vaudeville Performance that lifted the moral of his soldiers in England and France in 1944.

Through the discovery of her parents' letters, she has devoted her time to the USO of North Carolina while serving on their Board of Directors. Sarah is writing a book titled *Dearest Darling, Dearest Sweetheart,* that will feature the entire collection of her parents' love letters. Her book will include firsthand stories from her dad when she toured the battlefields of Europe with him and her mother's stories of struggles in raising their newborn son back home.

Sarah and her husband Nick currently live in Landfall and have two daughters, Olivia and Victoria.

Excerpt from
DEAREST DARLING, DEAREST SWEETHEART
Sarah Giachino

I never asked him if he ever killed anyone...that's a question one must never ask a veteran, but...I knew he did. How does one survive 210 days on the front lines in a war and then quietly return home to his wife and newborn son? How does one continue his married life after witnessing the horrors of war, then pick up where he left off managing a small hardware store chain and raising four children?

My dad, Charlie Hardman, was a typical rambunctious country boy who grew up in the rural mountains of West Virginia and helped save the world in 1944-45.

Charlie was an Army Infantry Soldier who fought the brutal Nazi regime from hedgerow to hedgerow through the hills of France continuing through Belgium, Holland, Germany and survived mortar wounds to return home in one piece. He is one example of thousands of men and women who stepped up to defend our country at a time when our fragile democracy was challenged in a global war.

His lifeline for survival during the long twenty-month deployment was the daily letters that he wrote to his wife, my mother, Mary. In 2001, I discovered a dusty old barrel-shaped basket tucked away in our family's home attic; it was full of their love letters. The recognizable vintage red-and-blue-edged airmail envelopes were tightly bundled, wrapped in twine and untouched since the day they had been tossed there. After asking my parents' permission to read them (after all, this was a very private chapter in their lives), they agreed and I soon discovered their incredible story of unconditional love, devotion and survival.

My mother wrote to my dad every single day and sometimes twice a day. Her letters were very detailed, describing her life raising their new baby son while living in Morgantown, West Virginia with her mother. She tried to fight back the "tearsies" from fear and loneliness by lovingly signing each letter with her magenta lipstick kiss. He would return her kiss and sign his letters by rekissing her lipstick imprint. Dad never disclosed in the letters his consistent dangerous combat conditions and even told her to ignore the notice from the War Department when he was injured in the Battle of Aachen because he never wanted her to worry. He got in big trouble with her for that.

But he did describe his arrival seven days later after D-day and the littered beach full of personal effects from soldiers after the Allied landing on Omaha Beach. He also wrote of liberating villages in Normandy, Holland and Belgium, meeting the civilians who cried when they saw his soldiers liberate and march in to their town, setting up command posts in an abandoned Nazi officer's home, a complete description of his foxhole and his daily life overseas - anything that wouldn't worry her. But most of all, he wrote to her about the day he saw his mail courier running toward him in a remote field shaking a Western Union Telegram with the announcement he had been waiting weeks to receive.

Monday, May 15, 1944 [Somewhere in England]

Dearest Darling,

At last Sweetie, I got the cable today and experienced a thrill such as I've never experienced before. Gee but it made me feel happy and proud. Oh Honey, I love you, I love you, I love you! As you know, I've been looking for that cable every day and when it did arrive I felt as if I were walking on air. I was out in the field training my men this afternoon when I noticed a man in the distance running towards us. He was waving something over his head as he ran and it took me a few seconds to realize that it was our mail clerk and he was bringing me out a cable. I guess I took off about that time and my men said I jumped completely over a fence and ran like a scared deer towards the mail clerk. When I reached him and got the cable I was all fingers and it seemed like ages before I could rip it open. Gee those wonderful words that were written there.

I ARRIVED. BOTH FINE. MOTHER AND I LOVE YOU - CHARLES STANLEY.

I feel like I could write many pages tonight but I have another problem tonight so I'll have to stop soon. On the problem, the men want to use the name "Charles Stanley" as the password so his name will be whispered amongst the hills and ravines of England.

Every speck of my love to you both-my family.

Yo Hubby

PS Great big bundles of love, hugs and kisses to you Honey and Daddy sends his love to our Sunny Boy.

Two days earlier my mother wrote him of the good news.

Saturday night, May 13, 1944

Dearest Sweetheart,

Mother brought out 3 letters from you today and as usual cheered me 100% Honey and of course now I'm waiting for the one that tells me you have heard about our baby. I know the strain of not hearing must have been terrible on you. And of course Charles Stanley was just an ole slow poke and took his good ole time about appearing on the scene. As soon as I get him home from the hospital, I am going to snip off a little of his hair (he really has some Honey) and send it in one of my letters.

Everyone in your family thinks the baby is the exact image of you. It really is true Darling-he looks so much like you. It would have been wonderful if you could only be here and see everything Darling. But this is impossible I guess. Always remember I love you with all my heart Honey.

Yo wifie

Waiting describes everything they endured throughout their separation. My parents lived through a period during a World War when their relationship was solely dependent on communication through waiting on letters from each other. Thousands of miles and months of separation never diminished their pure love for each other. My dad never lost sense of who he was and my mother never, ever gave up on him. They are part of the Greatest Generation and this is their story.

*There is no greater agony than bearing an
untold story inside you.*
Maya Angelou

Doris Chew was born and raised in Lower Manhattan in New York City. Her parents emigrated from China to the United States in the 1930s and 1950s. She attended Stuyvesant High School, SUNY at Stony Brook and New York University School of Law. She went on to practice law in Manhattan for twenty-five years, including at a prestigious Wall Street law firm and a major insurance company.

She and her husband, Bill Stewart, recently moved from Ridgewood, New Jersey to Wilmington, North Carolina. They have two beautiful daughters, Avery and Lindsay (ages 23 and 21 respectively), who were adopted from China and New York. Her daughters' Chinese names, when translated into English, mean "Beautiful Star" - one from the East and one from the West.

Doris is currently writing a memoir to show her daughters that life is a journey that has many different paths. She hopes to inspire her daughters to follow the call of their hearts and take those different - sometimes winding - paths to their destiny.

Written for My Daughters
GUNG-GUNG AND PO-PO: THEIR JOURNEY FROM CHINA TO AMERICA
Doris Chew

When Gung-Gung (my father, your grandfather) was a little boy, his father left Gung-Gung's mother in China and traveled to Malaysia. We never found out the details of why my grandfather left. Whenever the subject came up between Gung-Gung and Po-Po (my mom, your grandmother), it was whispered in hushed tones. I don't know whether it was because they didn't want the children to overhear or whether it was a topic of such great shame and embarrassment that it should only be spoken of in whispers. Being kids, we strained very hard to hear the bits and pieces of the story of what happened and this is what I know.

My father was born in 1914 in Foochow, a little farming village on the southeastern coast of China. In the old days of China, there were hundreds of tiny little villages where all the male heirs of families lived together in the village. When a couple gave birth to a son, the son would marry a girl from a neighboring village and they would live in the husband's village. Over the centuries, the village would be known as the "Lee" village or the "Wong" village or in Gung-Gung's case, the "Chew" village. The village would be made up of related male siblings and cousins and their male children and their families.

In old China, husbands in the village do not leave or divorce their wives. In fact, it was acceptable for the husband to have a second wife, especially if the first wife was unable to produce a male heir, and if they were wealthy, to have third, fourth or fifth wives.

In a poor farming village, it was uncommon for the husband to take on another wife and, even more unheard of, for the husband to leave his wife and his village, especially if the wife gave birth to a son. Couples in those days didn't get married for love. They got married to have sons to help with farming or the family business and to carry on the family name.

For Gung-Gung, not only did his father leave his mother, but he also left his village and China. Gung-Gung's mother was left behind with a young son in the Chew Village. It was shameful for her to return with her son to her own village, but it was also not possible to stay in the Chew Village. Back in those days, it was also very difficult for a young woman to remarry. Who would want to marry a woman who was previously married and with a child from another man? Moreover, it was thought that there must be something seriously wrong with the woman if the husband left her after she gave birth to a son! This must have been a terrible dilemma for Gung-Gung's mother.

So when a man from another village wanted to marry Gung-Gung's mother, she must have been really relieved and happy! Unfortunately, life is never that easy. The man was willing to marry

Gung-Gung's mother but she could not bring her son with her to his village. He did not want to raise a child from another man. Gung-Gung's mother had to choose between getting married or keeping her son. For a mother, it must have been an unbelievably tortuous decision to make. Gung-Gung's mother chose to remarry and leave her son behind with a distant cousin's family in the Chew village. I think she thought it would be the only chance for survival for both of them. Gung-Gung never saw his mother, or his father, again. He was only five years old.

Life for Gung-Gung growing up was not easy. Although the family that took Gung-Gung in didn't mistreat him, they also didn't accept him as one of their own children. They were poor farmers and Gung-Gung had to earn his keep. Gung-Gung grew up herding sheep from dawn to dusk. There was no extra money to send him to school so he never learned to read or write. It must have been difficult for Gung-Gung to see his cousins go to school every day while he went to herd his sheep.

Then things must have gone from bad to worse for Gung-Gung because China was undergoing a civil war and poor young boys were being recruited to fight. When Gung-Gung turned fifteen in 1929, he stowed away on a British ship that was docked in Foochow. With only the clothing on his back, Gung-Gung hid on the ship not knowing where it was going. When the ship finally docked, one of the workers told Gung-Gung that a neighboring ship in the port was a better ship to be on. Based on that fateful advice, Gung-Gung jumped onto the other ship and became a stowaway on a U.S. ship bound for America. I'm sure Gung-Gung had no idea where America was!

After World War II broke out and after the Chinese Exclusion Act (which prohibited Chinese from becoming U.S. citizens) was repealed in 1943, the U.S. Navy offered any illegal aliens the right to citizenship if they logged in a certain number of hours on active duty in the Merchant Marines. The U.S. Navy probably thought that it would be unlikely many illegal workers would survive the numerous transatlantic trips on an unarmed Merchant Marine cargo ship during the war, but the ones who did make it deserved to be granted U.S. citizenship.

Gung-Gung worked in the engine room in the U.S. Merchant Marines for almost twenty years. Gung-Gung's ship never got hit by enemy torpedoes despite the numerous transatlantic trips he made during World War II and the Korean War. He was granted U.S. Citizenship in 1950.

I sometimes think about how miserable Gung-Gung's life must have been for him to decide it would be better to take his chances with the unknown world than to live in the homeland that he knew. He was a young man, scared but courageous, who was not willing to accept his circumstances and was determined to forge his own destiny. It was a decision that changed the geographic direction of our family tree.

As is the traditional Chinese custom, when Gung-Gung turned thirteen years old, an "arranged" marriage was established between him and a female infant who had just been born in a neighboring village. That infant, my mother and your Po-Po from the "Ling" village, was arranged to marry Gung-Gung. Gung-Gung and Po-Po never met each other before marrying twenty-two years later.

You must be wondering right now how Gung-Gung and Po-Po met if he left China when he was only fifteen years old and she was still living in China. After Gung-Gung left China, he sent money back to Po-Po's family whenever possible for the next twenty-five years. That money enabled Po-Po's family to survive the Japanese invasion of China in the 1930s and the civil war in China. The Communists defeated the Chinese Nationalists in 1949. In 1951, Gung-Gung finally was granted approval for Po-Po to leave China to travel to Hong Kong. After leaving China for twenty-two years, Gung-Gung and Po-Po met for the first time in Hong Kong and were married on December 1, 1951. Gung-Gung was thirty-seven years old and Po-Po was twenty-four years old. Soon after, the borders were closed for travel into and out of China.

We all have great stories within us. Our children, will one day, appreciate every word we write…probably when we are long gone and they finally make the time to sit and read what we have written… and wish we were there to tell them in person and answer their questions. Your written stories are a part of you they can hold in their hand.
Anonymous

Sherry Roberts Highberger was born and raised in the Mountains of Virginia in 1947. At age twelve, she worked in a local canning factory. The owner didn't know what child labor laws were. Later she worked as a bookkeeper for a photo engraver, a bank, a Traffic-Civil-Criminal Court, a swimming pool company, three real estate agents in three states and has volunteered for a non-profit.

Married to a Coca Cola executive for thirty-five years, she has lived in seven states and four countries: England, Scotland, Canada and Denmark. Sherry has been honored to meet actors, athletes, CEOs, politicians, presidents and royals. She has traveled to China, Russia, Iceland, Hungary, Australia, Thailand, Scandinavia, and the Caribbean. She and her sister Donna inherited a 1,600-acre working family farm in North Carolina.

Sherry is fortunate to still have good friends everywhere, especially a group of ten friends in Shrewsbury, Massachusetts called the "Shoes" who have been friends for thirty-five years. Sherry's favorite hobby is genealogy and states that "it's never boring, but time consuming and will never be finished." Sherry is amazed that she is still so close to her thirty first cousins.

Ever since Charlotte Hackman, the founder of the Landfall Writers' Group, asked, "Do you want to write a book? Join us," Sherry has been hooked on writing. She believes each of the twelve members of the group are funny, intelligent and inspiring and it shows in their diverse stories.

The Title of Sherry's book is, *The Heroes in My Family: From The Revolutionary War to Iraq-Iran-Afghanistan.*

THE WITCH OF CHATTOKA:
A HALLOWEEN TALE
Sherry Roberts Highberger

This story began when my twelve-year-old great-niece, Kaitlin, and I drove around New Bern, North Carolina one day on our usual Discovery Adventure Sunday. The sky was dark and cloudy as we approached the old side of New Bern that had not been restored yet. It was a bad section of town with lots of burned out or abandoned buildings and houses.

There were commercial sections that had nothing left but large, flat, cement foundations. The buildings that had been on those spots were long gone. All of this section of town bordered the Neuse River. I imagine this area of New Bern was a thriving commercial center about 100 years ago.

As we drove down Craven Street, we were attracted to a large old building, leaning a bit to one side, with timbers holding up the balcony over the front door. Because of the boarded-up bay windows on either side of the front door, we suspected that this used to be the neighborhood store and probably a large apartment upstairs.

We walked around the entire building, trying to avoid all of the broken glass. There was a For Sale sign and a Historic Preservation sign nailed to the side of the building. It sat on a whole empty block, all by itself and was two blocks from the Neuse River. What stories that old building could tell! Except for hurricanes and floods, this was *prime real estate*! I wished I had some money.

As Kaitlin and I walked around the old building, an elderly lady mysteriously appeared, sitting on the porch of the old store in a rocking chair. We had not noticed her when we first approached the old building. We walked toward her very slowly.

"This building has secrets," she said as she rocked. A cold wind seemed to blow through us as she spoke . . . *and it was July*. "It all started many years ago, even before the building was here, back in the time of the Chattoka Indians . . . but never stopped."

She wasn't looking directly at us. It was almost as if she was talking to herself, lost in some other world. "Something very bad happened to a Chattoka Indian woman named NizHoNi-PoWaQa, when she went into the woods to pick berries to trade with the sailors. And that's how it started."

The old lady stopped talking and just rocked while we stood there, not knowing what to say.

"A little girl, who lived upstairs in this building, disappeared and was never found," she continued. Then thirty-three years later, another little girl who lived here with a different family disappeared and was never found, either. It scared a lot of people in the neighborhood.

People moved out. This block was almost deserted. It gets lonely here."

And then she looked directly at us, with eyes that felt like they could see right through us. "Are *you* interested in this old building?"

Suddenly we had the urge to leave the old section of New Bern.

That night, my three great-nieces Kaitlin and her cousins, seven-year-old Claire and four-year-old Emery, were spending the night with me in the New Bern Hotel. *They all thought they were the Eloise of the Comfort Suites.* As they got ready for bed, they begged me to tell them a scary story.

Kaitlin said, "Let's tell them about the scary old lady in the rocker, on the porch of the building. And the little girls, who have disappeared and were never found." *Aw, Kaitlin, let's scare your little cousins to death before bedtime, why don't ya.*

And that's how this story began; I have since done more research on Old New Bern. What follows are some of the ideas for a longer Halloween story of the same title, soon to be published.

October 31, 1667
Coastal Indian Village of the Chattoka, Province of North Carolina

The first ship from Europe comes in from the Atlantic between the barrier islands, up the Neuse River, to the Trent River. The captain sees the Chattoka Indian village and stops there. He sends two dories with sixteen men to trade with the Chattoka Indians for fresh water, meat, fruits and vegetables for their voyage back to Europe.

Two of the men see the most beautiful Chattoka woman. Her name is NizHoNi - PoWaQa. As she walks into the woods to pick berries to trade, they quietly follow and overpower her, accidently killing her. They panic. *What* have they done? If the Indians catch them, they will be killed and the captain will let them; he allows no nonsense from his men.

They dump her body in a swamp and pile large rocks on top of her so that she doesn't float to the surface. They return to the dories, help load them and are on the first dory back to the ship. The ship leaves and while crossing the Atlantic, a hurricane mysteriously overwhelms their ship and sinks it to the bottom of the sea with no survivors.

1698
Coastal Indian Village of the Chattoka, Province of North Carolina

About every ten years, a new ship discovers this little cove. Having been here once before, Swiss Captain Christof Graffen has brought settlers, including his wife Catharina and daughter Elsbeth to inhabit this new land. They "displace" the Chattoka Indians and take their land. He names the settlement "New Bern." He clears land by the port for a dock and warehouse and establishes his family's home on the top floor of the warehouse.

October 31, 1700
New Bern, Province of North Carolina

Catharina Graffen has sent little six-year-old, blonde, blue-eyed Elsbeth outside to play by herself; there are no other children in their small settlement. She could play with the Indian children *if* they were here today.

A dark cloud covers the sun, the sky turns black, a thick dense fog rolls out of the wooded swamp. It surrounds the store and warehouse . . . and Elsbeth. Just as suddenly as it came, it recedes back into the wooded swamp. No one notices. *Elsbeth is gone*!

Dinner is ready so Catharina starts calling Elsbeth from the window, but doesn't see her. She goes out and circles the building looking for Elsbeth but she is nowhere to be seen. Catharina walks the settlement, but no Elsbeth; no one has seen her.

Catharina walks down to the shore where the men clean their catch at the end of the day. She tells Christof that she cannot find Elsbeth anywhere and she's very worried. "Don't worry, my darling," he said. "She is just hiding. We will find her."

He looks everywhere Catharina has looked. No Elsbeth. He goes to the tavern and asks the men to help him find her. One suggests they try the Chattoka Indian village down the path. It's getting dark so they light torches and walk to the Chattoka village.

The elders are very sympathetic. They ask all of their children if they have seen the little girl with hair the color of the sun. The children smile because they like Elsbeth, but none of them have seen her today.

The Graffens and the villagers looked for Elsbeth every day, week and month, but Elsbeth was never found.

1702
New Bern, Province of North Carolina

Christof and Catharina stay for two more years and finally agree to sell everything and go back to Switzerland. She is afraid her new baby boy would disappear like his sister did.

1705
New Bern, Province of North Carolina

The store and warehouse sit empty for three years before a German businessman, Ernst Heinrich, buys it sight unseen. He wants to create a shipping company to transport goods in and out of the colonies.

1710
New Bern, Province of North Carolina

After five years, Ernst marries a pretty young widow, Madeleine, and they start their family quickly.

October 31, 1733
New Bern, Province of North Carolina

Within sixteen years, Ernst and Madeleine have six boys and a pretty little girl, Hansel. Seven-year-old Hansel loves to play with her older brothers, but sometimes they leave her behind. And today is no exception. So, she stays around the building and plays by herself.

The sun is blocked, the sky turns black. A thick fog rolls in around the store and warehouse and Hansel is engulfed. The fog quickly recedes into the wooded swamp. No one notices. *Hansel is gone*!

They look for months but Hansel is never found.

1755
New Bern, Province of North Carolina

Captain Baltasar de Castillo of Spain has sailed into this port many times. He sees the "For Sale" sign on the store and warehouse. He's getting tired of being away from his bride, Lucia, so he buys the building, loads his ship with supplies and heads back to Spain.

1756

New Bern, Province of North Carolina

A year later, Baltasar and Lucia arrive back in the settlement. *Some think it used to be called Chattoka, an Indian village, but it was probably a myth.*

1757

New Bern, Province of North Carolina

Baltasar and Lucia's little girl, Mariana, is born, soon followed by two boys and two girls. Mariana, as she gets older, is a big help with the little ones. Who will be next to disappear into the fog?

To be continued...

No matter what century, the fog will be back
every thirty-three years.
Hold tight to your young daughters or when
No one notices,
They Will Be Gone!

Happy Halloween!

MY FIRST KISS . . .
With a Boy Who Was Not My Cousin!
Sherry Roberts Highberger

I grew up in the mountains of Virginia. There were three mountains and two hollers (or "hollows" for you city slickers). Our dirt roads didn't have names, just tiny state-road numbered signs that the kids would steal. If people didn't know where you lived, they couldn't find you. There were about ten or fifteen kids living in the two hollers and up in the mountains.

We usually played with the kids next door. "Next door" meant three fields, one barnyard, one chicken house, and three to four fences between the two of you. If it was summer, you couldn't see the house "next door." We were the "Under the Arch" kids. This beautiful old concrete railroad arch, built in 1900, was the *only* way to get into our hollers. It's still standing today *and* it has a Historic Marker on it now.

Around the age of twelve, I decided that kissing a boy, whom I had been holding hands with all summer, might be coming up soon. Every night while in bed with the lights out and my younger sister sound asleep in the twin bed beside me, I would pucker up and kiss the backs of my two fingers; I was pretending they were his lips. After doing that for two weeks, I thought I was finally ready to do the real thing.

At about ten o'clock on a sunny July morning, the neighbor boy (who lived up the mountain holler on the left) and I were walking down the dirt road holding hands. Summoning my courage, I swung around to initiate the kiss but our feet and ankles got tangled and down we went! Caught totally by surprise, he got up, looked at me in shock and ran off . . . never to be seen again for the entire summer. When we returned to school in the fall, he pretended not to know me. Boy, oh boy!

My first kiss with a boy was a total disaster. So, I kept on practicing on my cousins.

A professional writer is an amateur who didn't quit.
Richard Bach

Anne Keeble is the daugher of a European couple who immigrated to Michigan in the early 1960s. German was her first language until she reached the age of seven, when she learned English in a Catholic school.

At the age of seventeen, she studied the literature of Goethe at Phillips University in Marburg, Germany and then earned a degree in marketing and hospitality from Central Michigan University. Specializing in promotional services for retailers, she built her own advertising business called Direct Promotions, based in Troy, Michigan. After twelve years, it was sold to a large conglomerate.

No longer on the fast track of corporate America where her late husband flourished, she now serves as a trained script supervisor, aiding directors with their commercials, episodic TV shows and feature movies.

For years, she has encountered numerous interesting characters with drama, comedy and endearing backgrounds. It's with careful selection that she pulls together their life experiences, creating non-fiction results on paper. Anne is especially tuned in to the special details about these people, written in her stories.

Deeply committed to her three grown children who live across the United States, Anne is regularly en route to their family gatherings. Back in Germany, she still has aunts, uncles and cousins, many in the teaching profession. Definitely a modern, global family unit.

AGAINST AUTUMN'S SKY
Anne Keeble

I wrote the following based on the experiences of my friend's father, with concluding thoughts from my friend.

Sometimes it vanished against the deep colors of the sky. The blue delta kite, trimmed with white, was a Father's Day gift given to me by my late wife Julie a couple years back. It launched easily and without much resistance, it reached the end of the 400-foot string. As planned, I let it go and we watched it float away freely over the Atlantic Ocean.

Julie had died exactly a year ago that afternoon. Our two kids stood with me, arms crossed, eyes squinting upward. This beach was where generations of my family vacationed. The kids frequently spent weekends here with friends during their college years.

My daughter's eyes lightly filled with tears, yet she managed to turn up the corners of her mouth, sending me a smile of approval. She shares the same dimples as her mother, the same copper blonde hair, but my deep blue eyes. Her tall, athletic brother isn't much different, though he has my stoic, broad shoulders that carry today's burdens.

Julie and I had become empty nesters, with plans to retire in ten years to this beach. Building her a dream home will remain only in blueprint, laying across my home office drawing board. As an aftermath, our house sold last week. Arranged by my son's friends, everything was moved into storage so I could continue searching, with a patient Realtor, for a new dwelling. Thus far, no house has felt like a home. None of this was going as planned. Julie always was the visionary. Now I'm faced with the consequences. Her decision, not mine.

Sadly, Julie became trapped in her own depressed darkness, unable to accomplish daily tasks. I did all our laundry. She no longer could be trusted behind the wheel of a car. Simply shopping for groceries had become a huge challenge. When I returned home from work and approached the driveway, it was always with hesitation, not knowing exactly what I'd be up against when I walked through the door but generally understanding that it would result in drama.

She no longer participated in her Bible group. Friends checked in on her often, but only by phone because Julie declined all their invitations to go out. Our family network was diligent in helping her find recovery. My devotion and dedication was endless and determined. It seemed she was "doing better" when in reality she found her strength for peaceful salvation with a gun.

Six months of counseling after her death was a process for the kids and me. We needed it desperately. The "new normal" became a pattern with each holiday, birthday and anniversary. We realized when the dates were approaching; we knew the routines and traditions and we made it through "the first" of everything together, without Julie.

For my own solitude, I needed to find a simpler way to escape from the sadness, whether through church, work or travel. I found some relief from my emptiness when a Christian mission group found me. It was started by an advertising CEO out of Chicago, who developed trips overseas to give aid to those less fortunate. My energies had found a rightful cause, though my children resisted giving their full support. The mission was in *need* of *me*. This could provide distraction from my grief and yet build our eternal justification, like a new retirement plan. It was new day, a new dawning - mine.

As I got off the plane in India, I was totally conspicuous. Arriving in the city of Hyderabad, I realized how different I was among the more than six million Hindu inhabitants. Within our group of nine, we had an Indian translator, and the rest of us were Caucasian. Hotel accommodations were "weak," yet we appreciated the running water and *sometimes* electricity, which I learned is a rare luxury.

Entering the modest lobby, we were introduced to Shyamali, our travel guide. Her smile and soft voice was an immediate connection of comfort for me. Acknowledging her Christian background was restricted, as she was commissioned to prayer lecturing only in private house churches. Widowed for two years after soldiers persecuted the church leaders for accepting financial relief from U.S. missionaries, her husband left her with nothing. That evening we shared conversations regarding our losses, discovering grief isn't partial and has no language barriers. I saw her tears, she saw mine.

In the morning of the second day, Shyamali's crew greeted us again in the lobby. They debriefed us of the intended goals. Boarding our vans, we were en route three hours, heading east along a dusty, gravel road. Overlooking mountain valleys, we approached multiple villages, shockingly poor, polluted and visually chaotic. Stopping frequently along the way, it was with great caution we were able to interact with the gallery of curious onlookers, wandering the street to watch a Christian group of vehicles drive through. Their curiosity was more than offset by the amazing warmth, hospitality and love from downtrodden "caste" people, who own almost nothing material.

The splendor of serene, sandy beaches and happy family dinners felt like planets away from what I witnessed in the large, black eyes of the children clinging to their mothers. The Indian culture governs religious worship only to Hinduism, forbidding the use of water sources and purchase of groceries to non-Hindus. It is a documented spirit within the Indian Constitution. The Christian villagers secretly pray to God, for fear of punishment. During our casual visits, their excitement was heightened by learning about America, along with discussions about Christian beliefs for one almighty God, rather than multiple Hindi gods.

For hours we shared about the gracious lifestyles we experience back in the United States. Strange, how patriotic and homesick I became through those conversations. Our following day was planned differently with a congregation of 400 people to meet down in the mountain valley, behind a fortress of stone walls. There we would split into three large groups.

My group included Shyamali as lead principal. An agenda was established to provide food to the mothers and their children while sharing God's love in anticipation of their faithful conversion. Laughter filled the air as candy was passed out to the little ones. Surprising to me, they did not gobble down the treats. Taking small parts off for a tasting, the remainder was gently rewrapped so they could take it home for others to enjoy. This courtesy is a survival technique, showing shared concerns to flourish in love.

Rumblings could be heard a close distance away. Misinformed, I was told the other mission group was loudly singing and dancing. Shyamali's eyes grew large with fear as she motioned me to turn and walk away from the group. Uncertain of her request, I headed toward her for clarification. The women began to scream and grabbed their children. Escalating fears quickly turned to chaos.

My instinctual reaction was to calm the group. Adrenaline causes my heart to rush beats, identical to those moments before Julie would panic during her unknown demons. A flood of thoughts filled me. *What can I do? How can I ease this?*

Standing stoic, yet with no answer, I watched a rush of soldiers break through into the madness. A machine gun was suddenly directed at my head. Blurred vision took over as I watched Shyamali converse with the soldier, her fearless attempt to negotiate my release. The authoritative soldier did not flinch, nor respond. It was my last sight of her. A new vision stood before me of Julie.

Sometimes it vanishes into the deep colors of the sunset. The bright red delta kite resists gently as I pull it back down from the sky. It was two years ago today that my Dad let his kite fly out over the ocean, symbolic of Mom's journey to heaven. My kite lands gently on the warm sand as my sweet wife runs over to gather it up in her arms. Mom never had the chance to meet the love of my life. I can't help smiling as I look at her cumbersome belly-bump jiggle as she runs toward the direction of my sister yelling, "I'm hungry; let's go eat."

With mesquite charcoal smoke filling the air, Dad removes the chicken and burgers off the grill. It's time to sit, say grace and enjoy our family dinner. So much has happened these past three years since we lost Mom. The journey forward has not been with ease, but we learned to take it one step at a time.

After Dad returned injured from his India mission, his stoic demeanor has vanished. Calmness has grown into his daily rhythm. Forever faithful to God and his family, Dad opens up more often about his life journey, though he doesn't discuss his mission work in India. His retirement phase is approaching quickly, and he has decided to resign from travel overseas.

Though lonely, he has not rushed the desire to replace Mom. Selfishly, I realize this allows me more time with him for myself. All I want is to become more like him. Dad forever is my hero.

My wife and I are filled with blessings as we await the birth of our son, due in six weeks. We are blessed to have a future with Dad; my son will grow up alongside his granddad, a namesake.

Together we will fly many more kites high above the ocean.

ACKNOWLEDGMENTS

To our spouses and families for their support and patience during production of this book, we are grateful.

We sincerely appreciate the encouragement and endorsements of Tom Morris and Clyde Edgerton.

To Diane Torgeson we owe admiration for the thoughtful cover design of our book. Indeed, we have all come together from separate lives to weave a book of our stories.

Thanks to Dick Nasca and Charlotte Hackman for many hours of organizing the material for this book.

Thanks to our editor Dalene Bickel.

LANDFALL WRITERS' GROUP 2016

Front row, L-R: Sherry Highberger, Doris Chew, DianeTorgerson, Ann Keebel, Dick Nasca
Back row, L-R: John Roper, Sarah Giachino, Carol Smith, Myrna Brown, Charlotte Hackman

Ed Hearn

Marie Gillis

CPSIA information can be obtained
at www.ICGtesting.com
Printed in the USA
FSOW03n0311171116
27466FS